USBORNE

Sandy Lane Stables

More great Sandy Lane stories
for you to read:

A Horse for the Summer

The Runaway Pony

The Midnight Horse

Dream Pony

Ride by Moonlight

Horse in Danger

The Perfect Pony

Racing Vacation

Strangers at the Stables

Michelle Bates

USBORNE

First published in 1996 by Usborne Publishing Ltd, Usborne House,
83-85 Saffron Hill, London EC1N 8RT, England.
www.usborne.com

First published in America August 1997. AE

ISBN 0 7945 0503 1 (paperback)

Typeset in Times

Printed in Great Britain

Editor: Susannah Leigh
Series Editor: Gaby Waters
Designer: Lucy Parris
Cover Design: Neil Francis
Map Illustrations: John Woodcock
Cover Photograph supplied by: HorsePix

With thanks to Ron Webster
(Training Manager, London Ambulance Paramedic Centre)

SANDY LANE STABLES

BARN →

GATE →

STABLE YARD

TACK ROOM

NICK & SARAH'S COTTAGE

POND

OUTDOOR SCHOOL

SANDY LANE

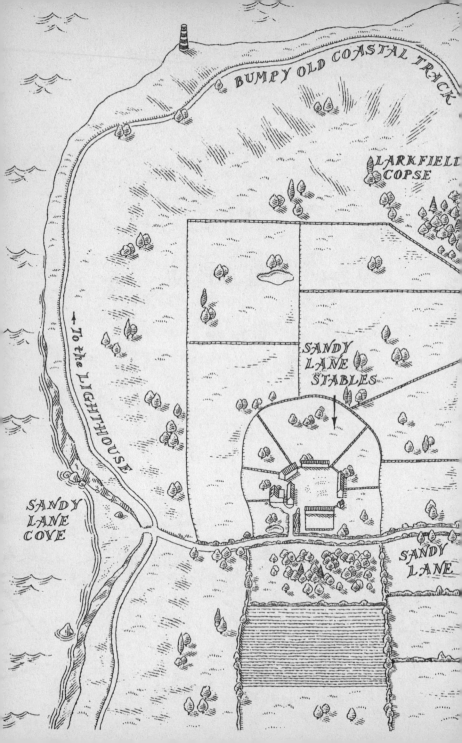

SANDY
BAY

BUCKNELL
WOODS

To ASH HILL

To
COLCOTT

PIG
FARM

CONTENTS

1

SOME BAD NEWS

"If we have to close down the stables, we'll close down the stables..."

Rosie Edwards just caught the end of the telephone conversation going on in the tack room and looked up, startled. Nick Brooks – the owner of Sandy Lane Stables – sounded unusually tense. As she watched him run toward the house, her stomach turned itself in knots.

What was going on? Surely Nick and his wife Sarah weren't thinking of packing it all in, not when things were just starting to take off? Why would they close down Sandy Lane? Questions rang in Rosie's head like alarm bells.

She felt uneasy. She hadn't been riding at Sandy Lane long, but already it was her life. It had been hard for all of her family, uprooting themselves with her father's job, but hardest of all for Rosie – new home, new school, new friends. It wasn't until she'd discovered Sandy Lane that she really started to feel settled. Here at the stables, she had made all of her friends, even her best friend Jess Adams. Rosie felt hot tears pricking her eyes as she remembered how awful it had been before she had known any of them.

Rosie walked over to the house and glanced in through the kitchen window. Nick and Sarah were talking inside and she could just catch the tail end of what they were saying. She wouldn't normally be caught dead eavesdropping, but this sounded serious.

"We'll have to discuss it with Beth immediately," Sarah was saying, as Nick paced up and down the floor. He had his back to the window, so Rosie couldn't catch his reply. Before Rosie even had time to step out of the way, the door had been flung open and Nick hurried out. Rosie jumped back, embarrassed.

"I didn't see you there. Are you OK, Rosie?" he said, breathlessly.

"Yes, fine Nick." Rosie swallowed hard. "What time do you want us in the outdoor ring?" she asked, quickly changing the subject.

"Sorry. What was that?" Nick looked up distracted.

"I was just asking what time..." Rosie started.

But her words were cut short as the ring of the telephone sounded around the yard and Nick rushed off to answer it.

Rosie sighed. Deep in thought as she crossed the yard, she saw Kate and Alex Hardy, two more of the Sandy Lane regulars, sprinting up the drive... late as usual.

"Morning, Rosie," they called.

"Morning," she answered.

On the other side of the yard, Tom Buchanan, Sandy Lane's star rider, sprang neatly into the saddle of his horse, Chancey. It was the start of the Spring break and everyone was in high spirits, but Rosie didn't feel like joining in. Putting on a brave face, she waved as she saw Jess ride into the yard.

"All ready for Tentenden training this morning?" Jess called.

"Sort of," Rosie answered flatly.

It was their first training session in preparation for the Tentenden Team Chase, and normally any mention of the cross-country race made Rosie feel better instantly. But this morning there were more important things to think about – would there even be a team, for instance, if Sandy Lane was to close down?

The day Nick had announced that she, Tom, Charlie and Jess would make up the team, had been one of the most important days of Rosie's life. She would be devastated if they couldn't enter now. Pulling back the bolt to Pepper's stall, she decided to put it out of her mind and stepped inside. Absent-mindedly, she ran the body brush over the pony's shoulder. Before she knew it, someone had crept up behind her and...

"BOO!"

Jess pounced on her.

Rosie nearly jumped out of her skin as Jess collapsed into fits of laughter.

"Jess, you frightened the life out of me," Rosie said, irritated. "Can't you take anything seriously?"

"Like what?" Jess asked, munching on a mouthful of apple.

"Well, if I tell you something... something awful," Rosie continued. Immediately, Jess looked concerned.

"Go on then. Spill the beans. Don't keep me in suspense."

And in a moment Rosie had blurted everything out... about the telephone call, Nick and Sarah's worried faces, her fears of the stables being closed down...

"What do you think it can mean, Jess?" Rosie asked at the end of it. "It sounds as though they're going to pack it all in."

"They wouldn't do that," Jess said quickly. "Nick and Sarah would never leave Sandy Lane. Besides, they'd tell us about it first, wouldn't they? Are you sure you heard things right?"

"Of course I did." Rosie shrugged her shoulders.

"Well, maybe Charlie knows something about it," Jess said, and quickly she called their friend over. "Charlie, Charlie."

Charlie Marshall looked up from where he was sweeping and ambled over. He listened carefully to what Rosie had to say, but he didn't seem to think it could be serious either.

"Tell her it's nonsense then," Jess begged, "or we'll never hear the end of it."

"It's nonsense," Charlie began. "But that doesn't mean..."

"Doesn't mean it's not true?" Rosie said coldly. "Why doesn't anyone ever believe me? It was like that time at Christmas when I tried to tell Charlie there wasn't any school the next day and he went in anyway," Rosie finished.

"Well, I admitted I was wrong then, didn't I?" Charlie said humbly. "I thought you were joking. Nobody told me the boiler had broken down and I was the one who looked stupid turning up at an empty

4

school. It's not that we don't believe you, Rosie. It's just that it seems so unlikely. I know Sandy Lane's had its tough times, but it's come through all that. Nick and Sarah have been doing so well lately, and they'd hardly have taken on a new stable girl if they were about to close down the stables, would they?"

Rosie looked unconvinced. "But don't you see, Charlie," she said in frustration, "I don't think this is something they've been planning. I think it's something awful that's just happened!"

"I give up with you two," Charlie groaned. "Stop panicking. Nick will tell us everything in good time. There's work to do. I'm going to tack up Napoleon."

"Yes, come on Rosie," said Jess. "We'd better get a move on if we're going to get our horses ready."

"Look, here's Nick right now," said Charlie, seeing Nick stride across the grounds. "Let's ask him what's going on."

"No... no don't do that," Rosie said urgently. "It'll look as though I was listening in on them."

"Well, you were weren't you?" Charlie said grinning.

Rosie shot him a dirty look. "I don't want Nick to know that," she whispered, in an annoyed voice.

"Fair enough," Charlie said. And before he had a chance to say anything anyway, Nick began talking.

"I'll be taking the training session at eleven," he called, "and I need to see everybody in the tack room at twelve. Can you spread the word? I've got some important news... news that's going to affect all of you, I'm afraid. And if you see Beth, can you tell her to come and find me at the house?"

"See," said Rosie as Nick hurried off. "I told you.

5

Sandy Lane's going to be shut down."

"Oh, come on Rosie," groaned Charlie. "Stop being so dramatic."

"Well, I think we ought to tell the others what Rosie's heard anyway," said Jess. Charlie shrugged his shoulders. "It's only fair that everyone knows," she continued.

Charlie nodded. "OK then. I suppose you're right."

Rosie grimaced as Charlie and Jess disappeared. It wouldn't take long for the news to get around.

"Whatever are we to do Pepper?" she asked the little black and white pony as she quickly went over his coat with the body brush.

"Talking to yourself Rosie?" Beth's smiling face appeared over the door of Pepper's stall.

"There you are, Beth. Nick's been looking for you," Rosie said. "He wants you to meet him at the house with Sarah."

"Sounds serious. Hope I'm not about to get the boot!" Beth smiled.

Rosie felt quite uncomfortable. Beth was the new stable girl. She hadn't been at Sandy Lane long, but she had fit in right away. Rosie had been worried when Nick had told them he was employing someone to help out... worried that she would try to take over. But as soon as Rosie had met Beth, she knew she needn't have worried, Beth wasn't like that. She was more like a friend really. She was kind, not bossy at all, and absolutely amazing with the horses. Rosie couldn't help liking her.

Making her way across the yard, Rosie collected Pepper's saddle from the tack room. Word of her news must have gotten around already, for her friends were

6

looking very gloomy. Anxious to escape another postmortem of Nick's words, Rosie hurried back to Pepper's stall. She patted Pepper's shoulder and tacked him up, leading him over to join the others. Tom, Charlie and Jess were already making their way down to the outdoor ring.

"All here?" Nick called distractedly as he opened the gate and let everyone in.

"I want everyone to start by mounting and dismounting correctly on both sides," he called. "Then start walking around. I'll let you know when I want you to trot on. I'd like to see some turns on the forehand from a halt, rising trot on each diagonal and cantering on the lead I call out. Are you all ready for that?"

"OK," he went on when no one answered. "Tom, you start."

Tom led the way around the perimeter of the ring and Rosie brought up the rear. She was trying desperately to keep her mind on her riding. But Pepper was fidgeting and she knew she wasn't really concentrating. She looked across at the others. Charlie was frowning and didn't seem able to get Napoleon to respond, and Storm Cloud was napping with Jess.

"Come on everyone," Nick called. "Pay attention."

"One two, one two, one two," Rosie chanted, trying to stop Pepper from trotting into the back of Chancey.

After twenty minutes of warming up their horses, Nick didn't look terribly impressed.

"I think everyone's blundered through those exercises enough for now. Let's try some jumping."

Rosie looked anxiously at the course laid out in front of them. The jumps weren't that high, but she felt all jittery.

"All ready?" Nick called out. "Charlie, do you want to start and show us how it's done?"

"Sure," said Charlie, and with a flourish of his whip, he turned Napoleon to the first jump. Rosie held her breath. They were going very fast as they flew over the brush and cantered on to the stile. They soared over the next two fences in swift succession, but Charlie wasn't going to jump clear. As he turned Napoleon to the gate, the little bay firmly refused, and although Charlie turned him three times, he still couldn't get him to jump it.

"Try him over the parallel bars to relax him," Nick called, and quickly Napoleon went on to clear them.

Rosie watched grimly as Tom took a turn at the course and knocked down two jumps. And Jess did no better, knocking down three.

"My turn," she muttered to herself, trying to focus her attention on the course ahead of her, as Nick called her forward. She gritted her teeth and kicked Pepper on for the brush. But her mind was elsewhere, and although she jumped clear, she knew it had been a slow round.

"That's enough for one day," Nick said at the end of the session. "I don't know what's wrong with you guys. I haven't seen such laborious riding in a long time. You'll have to work harder if you're going to be ready for Tentenden – it's only four weeks away. And don't forget – everyone's to meet me in the tack room in five minutes time." He turned on his heel as he spoke and strode out of the ring.

Gloomily, Rosie led the way back to the stables, taking Pepper to his stall. She was furious with herself. She hated riding badly in front of Nick.

Impatiently, she fumbled with Pepper's girth as she tried to undo the buckle. "More haste, less speed," she muttered under her breath. "And you can take that look off your face too, Pepper," she snapped, closing the stall door behind her. "I'll be back later to sponge you off."

She knew she should really do it right away but the news in the tack room simply couldn't wait. Slinging the saddle across her arm, she hurried inside and hung the saddle up on its rack before she sat down. Nick looked serious as he sat leaning against the desk, his arms folded in front of him.

"Are we all here now?" he asked.

Rosie looked around at the expectant faces. Tom was there and Charlie too. Even Alex and Kate had managed to turn up on time. This was important news after all. Jess gave Rosie a 'don't worry' kind of look as she shifted uneasily in her seat.

"I'll come straight to the point," said Nick. "Sarah and I have had some bad news."

Rosie's heart skipped a beat. She sat rooted to the spot. This was it, he was going to tell them it was all over for Sandy Lane.

Nick glanced across at his wife and took a deep breath before he went on. "I'm afraid Sarah's dad has been taken ill. He's had a heart attack and has been rushed into the hospital."

The news was greeted by low mutterings, followed by an embarrassed silence.

"He's all right," Nick went on. "But he needs time to recover. He's going to be in the hospital for a while and, in the meantime, we've agreed to go and run his stud farm for him in Kentucky."

Rosie felt a wave of relief flood through her. So Sandy Lane wasn't closing down forever. Then, almost immediately, she felt terrible. How could she have been so selfish? Sarah's father was ill, and all she could think about was the future of her beloved stables.

"We've asked Beth to take charge of Sandy Lane while we're away," Nick went on. "At the moment we'll be gone for three weeks, but obviously we'll get back sooner if we can. Beth's going to come and live in the house until we get back. And I was kind of hoping that you lot might offer to help out. It is the start of the Spring break after all. And I'd feel a lot happier knowing you were giving Beth a hand down here. What do you say?"

"Of course we'll help out, Nick," said Tom, taking charge of the situation. "There's no question of that, is there?" He turned to look at the others. His friends all nodded in immediate agreement.

"When are you going?" Tom asked, turning back to face Nick.

"Well," Nick sighed heavily. "We've managed to get flights for Monday morning which doesn't give us long to get everything organized – just two days." His voice trailed off as Sarah started to speak.

"You'll have to bear with us. There's going to be a lot to sort out before we go. It's going to be a tough few days for everyone." She smiled weakly.

"We should be back in time for the Tentenden Team Chase, but Beth has agreed to continue with the training," Nick continued. "I'll set up a program with her before I go. I'm sure everything will be fine, but I'll leave you our number in Kentucky, as well as a contact number of a friend of mine in case of emergency." Nick smiled anxiously. "I'm sure you won't need them. You should be fine with Beth in charge."

Not knowing what else to say, Rosie and her friends trooped out of the tack room and tried to busy themselves around the stables.

2

THEY'RE OFF

Sarah wasn't wrong in saying it would be a tough few days for them all. There was so much to organize. Schedules had to be written for mucking out, feeding and grooming. Lessons and rides had to be decided upon. Routines had to be established. In the end it was decided that it would be easier if the regulars were responsible for two horses each and, while Beth would take all private lessons, the regulars could lead rides.

Eventually, Monday morning arrived. By nine, the last of the bags were squashed into a taxi and Nick and Sarah climbed in. They were off.

"I've pinned the phone numbers on the tack room bulletin board," Nick called out of the window. "We'll call when we get there, but don't panic if you don't hear much from us. We're going to be very busy. Anyway, you'll be fine with Beth in charge."

"Sure, we'll be fine," Beth smiled. "What can

possibly go wrong in three weeks?"

"Practice hard," Sarah called as the taxi rolled out of the yard. "And don't forget to send off the Tentenden entry form!"

"Bye-eee..." the voices died away as the car disappeared down the drive and out of sight.

Rosie made her way to the water trough. Hunching her shoulders in the wind, she crossed the stable grounds, struggling under the weight of the water buckets. It was a gray, blustery April day. Rosie's teeth chattered as she gave the horses their buckets and pulled down the sleeves of her sweater. She stopped for a moment, scraping her blonde hair into a tight ponytail before strolling off to take another look at the cross-country course.

Rosie knew it like the back of her hand. She'd spent long enough helping Nick set it up over the winter months. They all had.

"Without our own cross-country course to practice over, we won't stand a chance at Tentenden." Nick's words echoed in Rosie's ears as she thought back to the day he had started to plan it all. Although the jumps weren't all that high, the course he had set up was a challenging one and each fence would have to be jumped clean, or the horse would be penalized. Standing on top of the little hill by the gate, Rosie's eyes narrowed as she took it all in and a rush of adrenaline ran through her. Absentmindedly, she gazed into the distance when a voice from behind her disturbed her thoughts.

"I've been looking for you everywhere. Did you forget we have a Tentenden training session?"

Rosie spun around to see Jess, walking toward her.

"How could I?" Rosie said, looking at her watch. "I was just checking out the course. Come on, let's go," she said, smiling.

The two friends chattered excitedly as they hurried back to the stables. Rosie collected her riding hat and made her way to Pepper's stall. The little piebald sniffed the air feverishly as Rosie folded back his blanket and started to tack him up. Attaching the breast plate to the saddle, she led Pepper out of his stall to join the others.

Rosie sprung nimbly into the saddle and nudged the little pony on through the gate at the back of the stables, into the fields behind. A gusty wind was blowing and it was drizzling with rain. Rosie's cheeks felt flushed as she drew Pepper to a halt under the trees.

"Here we all are. Excited?" Beth asked, reaching for her field binoculars. "As this is the first time I've taken you over the course, I'm not going to time you. It's pretty slippery, so just concentrate on getting around safely. OK?"

"Yes Beth," came a chorus of voices.

"Let's get going before it pours down. Try to be extra careful through the woods. There are a lot of branches lying around from last week's storm. I don't want your horses to spook. The most important thing is to take things slowly. The jumps aren't that difficult. Now, you all know where you're going, don't you?" she said.

"Yes Beth," they chorused.

"OK, Charlie, you go first followed by Jess, Tom and then Rosie," said Beth.

Rosie didn't know whether to feel pleased or

disappointed. She didn't want to go first, but at the same time, she thought she would die waiting for her turn. Rosie watched closely as Charlie rode across the field and approached the first jump. He was so quick, she envied him his speed. She would see him up to the trees, then she would go and warm up.

She turned Pepper to a quiet corner of the field and started to trot the pony around. Then she pushed him on into a gentle canter. Pepper had such a smooth, rhythmical stride, he was a pleasure to ride. Soon Rosie began to relax. She didn't realize how quickly the time had gone. When she returned to the group, Jess was already back and Tom was halfway around the course.

"How was it, Jess?" Rosie asked.

"Great," her friend answered, her eyes glinting brightly. "Storm Cloud was amazing. Weren't you?" She leaned forward, shivering as the coastal rain swept in across the fields.

And then Rosie heard Beth call her name. Gritting her teeth determinedly, she turned Pepper to the start. Her skin felt taut as the wind whistled past and Pepper lengthened his stride. Rosie squeezed him forward with her heels and the pony jumped over the tiger trap as if it was on fire. As Rosie steadied him before the brush, she felt a tremor run through his body. They took the fence in their stride and raced on toward the hayrack.

"Steady now Pepper. Easy does it," she crooned. "It's not as hard as it looks – it's only a hayrack."

Rosie sat deeper in the saddle and collected Pepper for the spread. Pepper snatched at the reins, impatiently waiting for Rosie to release him for the jump. Quickly, she urged him on, letting the reins ease through her fingers as the pony jumped clear and went on to soar over the hedge. Leaning forward as they entered the trees, Rosie swung Pepper toward the tree trunk. Determinedly, she urged him on. Without hesitating, Pepper rose to the challenge, up and over and on to the log pile.

Rosie knew they were going well. Bravely, Pepper gathered his legs up under him and they flew over the tires. Galloping forward, clear of the water jump, they approached the zigzag rails. Rosie held her breath. But they jumped it squarely, and the gutsy little pony landed lightly and went on to race over the gate. Rosie felt herself slipping and gripped harder with her knees as they thundered across the fields. The rain was pouring down now as they took the stone wall. Touchdown! They had done it. They had finished.

Pepper snorted, his breath spiraling from his nostrils like clouds of smoke, as Rosie slowed his pace to a trot.

Everyone was making so much noise when Rosie eventually returned to the group, that she couldn't get a word in edgeways.

"Quick everyone," Beth said, "we'll have to hurry back to the stables if we don't want to get drenched."

As the horses wound their way back into the stable grounds, Rosie felt content. She was soaked through to the skin, but somehow it didn't matter. Leading Pepper into his stall, she removed his tack and started to rub him down. Then she hurried to the tack room to get some grooming things. She could hear trouble brewing between Tom and Charlie over who was riding Hector and Napoleon in the afternoon rides. Putting her head over Blackjack's stall door, she glanced inside. Susannah – one of the younger pupils – was there with him.

"Did you enjoy your ride?" Rosie asked her.

"Yes," she replied. "Alex told me I was really improving," she added proudly.

"I'm sure you are," Rosie said kindly. "If you run to the barn and get Blackjack's food, I'll take over grooming him if you like."

"Thanks. I think my mom's waiting for me," Susannah answered gratefully, running off. Rosie picked up the body brush and got started on Blackjack's mottled coat.

"Keep still, Blackjack," she muttered.

"Here's his food, Rosie." Susannah's head appeared over the door.

"Great," Rosie said. "See you the same time next week then."

"Thanks," Susannah shouted over her shoulder as she ran off.

Impatiently, Blackjack shifted his weight as he eyed the food sitting outside the stall. Gently, he nosed Rosie's back as a little reminder that he was waiting.

"Don't you fret," said Rosie. "I haven't forgotten you, but you can't have your lunch till I have you clean. There, that should do the trick." She bent down to pick out Blackjack's last hoof. Patting his hindquarters, she closed the door behind her. That was her two horses done. She hoped Jess had gotten Storm Cloud and Minstrel settled as quickly. After all, they did have plans for that afternoon.

"All set, Jess?" Rosie cried as she saw her friend scurry past.

"Nearly," said Jess. "I'll check on Storm Cloud and then I'll be right with you."

Five minutes later they were ready. Looking at her reflection in the glass of the tack room window, Rosie wiped the smudges from her face.

"Come on," Jess urged, "or we'll be late."

Jogging down the lane, the girls headed for the bus stop at the corner of Sandy Lane. Out of breath and red in the face, they stumbled to the stop and climbed aboard the bus."

"Whew. We nearly missed it, slow poke!" Jess teased. "Two to Colcott, please," she said, digging around for some change.

The two girls chattered excitedly as the bus climbed the hill away from the coast. Fields of greenery sped past and buildings sprang up as the bus wound its way along the winding back roads.

As they neared the town of Colcott, the girls rang the bell. The doors swished open and Rosie and Jess jumped to the ground. The bus drove off, leaving them outside the old saddle shop.

"Afternoon Jess... Rosie."

Mr. Armstrong's jovial face peered out at them from behind the counter. The Sandy Lane regulars spent so much time in his shop, he had come to know all of their names. His watery blue eyes twinkled at his two favorite customers.

"They're ready, girls. I hope these are what you wanted."

The girls grinned at each other as Mr. Armstrong placed four brand new riding cap covers, in Sandy Lane red and black colors, on the shop counter.

"Yes, Mr. Armstrong," Jess breathed. "Those are just what we wanted. What do you think Rosie?"

"They're great Jess. We'll look like a real team now.

I can't wait to see the others' faces."

"Don't they know you've ordered them?" Mr. Armstrong asked.

"No," Jess said mischievously. "Rosie and I have been saving up for them for ages. We wanted it to be a surprise."

"And how are Nick and Sarah?" Mr. Armstrong asked, as he totaled what they owed.

"Haven't you heard?" Rosie said, glancing anxiously at Jess. "They're away at the moment. Sarah's father is sick." She paused to draw breath. "So they've had to go to Kentucky to run his stud farm for him. We're helping Beth look after Sandy Lane while they're away."

Mr. Armstrong looked concerned. "How long are they planning to be away for then? Is it serious?"

"I'm afraid it is," said Rosie. "He's had a heart attack. They're going to be away for three weeks."

"Well, if you speak to them, send them my best wishes," Mr. Armstrong said, looking worried.

Rosie nodded. "Come on, Jess. We'd better get going," she called over to where Jess was browsing through the bridles. "We'll miss the next bus back if we don't hurry, and we need to get the horses groomed and tacked up for the afternoon rides."

"Coming," said Jess. "Bye Mr. Armstrong," they called as they let themselves out of the shop. The low rumble of the bus sounded in the distance as Rosie and Jess waited patiently by the stop.

"Don't worry. We'll be at the stables soon," Rosie said as the bus pulled over and the two girls climbed on.

Twenty minutes later, the bus stopped at Sandy Lane

and Rosie and Jess jumped off. Rounding the corner by the sycamore tree, they walked on up the drive to the stables. Quickly, Rosie made her way to Pepper's stall, only to find it was empty.

"Uh oh," she said to herself. "Too late."

Jess looked equally sheepish as she met Rosie in the middle of the yard.

"Someone seems to have beaten us to it, Jess," Rosie said. "We're not going to be in anyone's good books at this rate."

"We couldn't help it," Jess said briskly. "Besides, we're not that late. Wait till the others see what we've got for them. They won't be mad then."

"I hope so," said Rosie, unconvinced. "Let's go and find them."

Eagerly they hurried to the tack room.

"Hi everyone," Jess called to a wall of stony faces.

"Nice of you to drop by." Charlie was the first to break the awkward silence.

"Sorry," Rosie mumbled. "We didn't realize we'd been so long."

"Obviously," Charlie said sarcastically.

"It's not very responsible to disappear on the first day Nick and Sarah are away," Tom said in a more appeasing voice. "We've all had to help get your horses tacked up."

"Oh... um... sorry," said Rosie, shamefaced.

"We've got to pull together while Nick and Sarah are away," Kate added, crossly.

"We know all that," Jess answered. "We're not trying to get out of our jobs. It's just that we had to pick up some things," she said.

"What things?" Charlie asked, frowning.

"These," said Jess, pulling the bag out from behind her back. "Hopefully they'll make you less annoyed with us. We bought them for Tentenden."

The colorful cap covers spilled out onto the tack room desk. Everyone stood back, looking embarrassed.

"Well, it's a good idea," Alex said kindly.

"Oh Jess, Rosie. They're perfect. You'll all look really professional," Kate exclaimed.

"Yes, thanks you two," said Tom, running the silk cap covers through his fingers. Charlie grunted noncommittally.

"You might be a little more excited," Jess said. "We went to a lot of trouble to get them."

"And they are very nice," said Tom. "It's just that there were only four of us to get the horses ready and Beth's lesson was late. We thought you'd just gone off and left everyone to do your jobs."

"Well thanks. Thanks a lot everyone," Rosie said huffily. "We didn't think you'd miss us for an hour and we wanted it to be a surprise."

"It was a surprise," Tom said appreciatively. "Come on you two," he said, linking arms with the two girls as he led them out of the tack room. "Don't look so upset. It's just that for a while, we've got to put the running of Sandy Lane above everything else – even Tentenden."

3

DISASTER STRIKES

"Don't let him puff out his belly when you're trying to tighten up the girth, Jess," Charlie called from the other side of the yard.

"I know that," Jess snapped. "But it's easier said than done. You're not the boss around here anyway. You know how Minstrel hates being tacked up. Why don't *you* put on his saddle if you think you can do any better!"

Rosie groaned. Not another fight. It had only been four days ago that they had waved goodbye to Nick and Sarah and already the arguments were in full swing – who was riding who, who was taking the lead, who was in charge of what. On and on it went. And it was getting worse. Yesterday they had all been bickering so much that one mother had lifted her child off Horace before the lesson had even begun.

Somehow, without Nick and Sarah around to

oversee the yard, things weren't quite so straightforward. Rosie liked Beth, but she just couldn't keep control like Nick did. Jess, for instance, was supposed to be in charge of Minstrel, but when Alex had brought him in from the trail ride yesterday afternoon absolutely plastered in mud, she had gone crazy and refused to groom him. And nothing Beth had said would make Jess change her mind.

"If you were the one who had to groom him, you wouldn't have let him get that dirty," Jess had screamed at Alex. Rosie cringed as she remembered the scene.

They weren't getting anything done on time either. Rosie looked at her watch. It was five after eleven. Beth was supposed to have started the lesson in road-work at eleven o'clock and Pepper was the only one of the horses ready.

"Come on everyone," Rosie moaned. "I must have circled Pepper at least a dozen times. He'll have made his own track if I'm not careful."

Jess scowled as she tried to help a rider with a leg-up onto Napoleon. "Coming," she grumbled.

By eleven fifteen, Jester, Napoleon, Minstrel, Storm Cloud and Whispering Silver stood groomed, tacked up and ready to go.

"At last," Rosie mumbled under her breath.

"Who's going on this ride, Rosie?" Beth called.

"The group training for their road-work test – George, Melissa, Anna, Mark and me," Rosie answered cheerfully.

"Excellent," Beth smiled. "All good riders. That should be fun. Let's go then," she said happily. "Follow on after me."

Rosie nudged Pepper forward, relieved to be leaving

the others behind her to argue things out. As the horses meandered down the tiny winding lane, Rosie thought what a fine spectacle they made. Their buffed coats gleamed as the April sun peered through the clouds. Beth and Whispering Silver led the string of horses and Rosie took up the rear. Slowly, they picked their way along the grassy verge of the roadside, past gates and hedges heading for the open fields ahead of them. Rosie pushed Pepper on into a brisk trot to catch up with Napoleon.

The farther they rode from the stables, the better Rosie started to feel. Of course it wasn't the same at Sandy Lane without Nick and Sarah around. She shouldn't have expected it to be really. But once things had settled down, they would be all right, she was sure of it. Rosie sighed contentedly as the wind rustled through the trees, stirring the leaves. The smell of the countryside enveloped her. It was so peaceful and the rest of the school break lay ahead of her to be spent at Sandy Lane.

Rosie didn't know when it was that she first heard the sound of the approaching car. Certainly it wasn't until it was right upon her as there were no warning calls from the front. It all happened so quickly. One moment, she was quietly ambling along the side of the road, the next, the low-slung red sports car had sped out of the Colcott junction and was heading straight for them at full throttle. Swiftly, she collected her reins and checked Pepper, but the riders ahead of her seemed to be having trouble as their horses danced skittishly from side to side.

Any minute now the car will slow down, Rosie thought to herself. But if anything, it seemed to accelerate. Rosie looked on in horror as the car swerved out of control across the road. At the last moment it careened left, not a hair's breadth away from the horses, and sped on. Rosie gasped as everything was thrown into total chaos. And later, when she was to look back on things, she couldn't remember anything very clearly. Horses and riders spun in a whirlwind of colors, shrieking voices and clattering hooves merged as one.

Rosie sat shell-shocked. She felt as though she was looking at a video that had been freeze-framed. Storm Cloud pirouetted in staccato movements, cannoning into the stampeding horses and then Whispering Silver reared, her eyes rolling in sheer terror, her legs flailing in the air as Beth clung on for dear life. Crash! In one split-second, Whispering Silver's shoes struck pavement and Beth was flung sideways from the saddle. There was a sickening crunch as Beth hit the ground. Whispering Silver thundered off down the road, taking horses and riders with her. Suddenly, Rosie snapped to her senses.

"Pull on the reins! Try to turn them back!" She shouted instructions until she was blue in the face, but it was too late. Napoleon was the only horse left behind, and George was struggling to keep him under control. Jumping to the ground, Rosie rushed over to where Beth had fallen. She felt the panic rising in her throat as she looked at the pale face of the girl stretched out on the ground, her leg twisted awkwardly underneath her.

"She's dead!" George screamed.

"No she's not," Rosie said as she felt for Beth's pulse. "She's unconscious, but there's a very definite beat. We need help. Can you ride and phone for an ambulance? I'll stay here with her. Tie Pepper to that tree over there."

"Beth, Beth. Can you hear me?" She turned back to the girl, not waiting for an answer from George.

"Go on," Rosie said. "There's a house some way up on the left. I can't remember the number, but it's got a white gate. Call Tom at Sandy Lane too. Tell him what's happened. Get him to come out and look for the others. And hurry," she said urgently.

Rosie watched as George turned Napoleon up the road toward Ash Hill, and galloped away into the distance. Quietly, she bent over Beth, stroking her hair, talking to her all the time, not knowing what to say.

"You're going to be all right," she whispered. "It was only a little fall. It looks worse than it is. Please, please be all right," she said. But there was no reply from the white, immobile figure laid out beside her. It had started to rain now. Big drops of water ran in rivulets down Rosie's back as she took off her coat and laid it over Beth to keep her warm. She didn't know what else she could do. She felt so helpless kneeling there, waiting and waiting. Beth groaned as Rosie leaned over.

"Beth... Beth can you hear me?" Beth opened one eye and groaned faintly.

"It's... it's my leg," she murmured.

"It's OK. It's OK," Rosie said, patting her hand. "They'll soon be here."

She looked at her watch. It could only have been five minutes ago that George had left for help, but it felt like ages. She thought she could hear something. Was it the sound of an engine in the distance? Her heart leapt as she jumped to her feet and then it sank again. Her mind was playing tricks on her. She grimaced as the sound faded away. Then she heard another noise and, as she stared into the distance, she could see a horse and rider cantering toward her. Rosie waited patiently as the figures got nearer and nearer. She breathed a sigh of relief. It was George.

"The ambulance is on its way." The words tumbled from the boy's mouth. "They should be here any minute. And I phoned Tom... he's coming out with Alex... how is she?"

"She's come to," Rosie said. "Her leg's hurting her, but I..." And then Rosie jumped up. There was a siren in the distance, getting louder and louder.

"The ambulance!" George cried, jumping off Napoleon.

Before Rosie knew it, an ambulance had appeared around the corner and everyone sprang into action. Neon lights flashed as three men jumped out and rushed over.

"What's her name?" one called.

"Beth. She's called Beth." Rosie answered weakly, watching them as they unloaded a trolley from the ambulance.

"Pulse is OK," she heard one of them mutter to the others, laying his hand against her brow.

"Temperature OK."

Rosie felt a wave of relief flood through her. Beth was groaning.

"Do you hurt anywhere?" one of them was asking her.

"She said something about her leg," Rosie intervened.

he ambulance man said kindly,
e others to get something. Rosie looked
hed a support bandage to Beth's leg.
men rolled her onto a board and
to the gurney.
ns now?" Rosie asked.
her to emergency... to Barkston
of them said. "Can you phone her

her mother," Rosie said.
hospital and get them to call the
ambulance man. "Wait till they get
you what to do," he said, heading
at.
id miserably, shivering as she shifted
foot to the other.
kly as the men strapped her to the
d her into the back, and then the
ff leaving Rosie and George
side waiting. It had all happened

rs should be here any moment,"
t, there they are now."
around and looked back in the
ne to see Tom and Alex running

e. Is Beth OK?" Tom asked, striding

ned off to Barkston emergency
s at least conscious when they took
hurting her," Rosie answered,
of a rather impatient Pepper who
ically at the ground.

"We must phone Beth's mother as soon as we get back and tell her she's been taken to Barkston," Alex said sensibly. "Are you all right, Rosie?"

"Yes, I'm fine," Rosie said, looking down at her disheveled appearance. "Just a little shocked. The police are on their way. I can't get over it... the car didn't stop. It must have seen the trouble it caused. Beth could have been killed and yet it didn't stop."

"Did you get its license plate?" Tom asked.

"No," Rosie cried. "It all happened so quickly. It was a red sports car... a man driving it, but everything else is a little hazy."

"What about you, George?" Tom asked.

"I'm afraid it's a complete blur," he answered, shaking his head.

"We've got to find the others," Tom said, suddenly taking charge of the situation. "You wait here for the police. Which way did they go?"

Rosie pointed vaguely in the direction of Ash Hill.

"Don't worry. We'll go and look for them. I'm sure we'll find them," said Tom, confidently. "We'll take Pepper and Napoleon off your hands. Just tell the police what you can remember."

Rosie watched as the two boys mounted the horses and disappeared into the distance. The police didn't take long to get there and soon Rosie found herself going over the events once more.

"I'm Officer Dale," the first policeman said as he strode over. "Can you tell me what's happened here?" he asked kindly. "The hospital radioed that there had been an accident."

"Yes, yes there was," said Rosie hurriedly. "The ambulance has taken Beth away – the girl who was e," she explained.

riders then?" he asked. "I was
of you down here."

ie paused for breath. "The horses
Our friends have already gone
told them which way to go...
ur horses..." The words tumbled
'We were just waiting for you
to the stables."

u long... just a few details, then
e policeman said, opening a
ned as he drew a map of the

r come from?"
on over there," said Rosie. "And

hit anyone?"
itantly. "But it drove very close

ugh it speeded up," George

would you estimate it was going
to George
otful. "It's hard to say. It just
said.

orses on the road?" he asked,

sie paused to draw breath. "We
road safety exams, so we
ny other way."

Officer Dale. "And how many
vehicle?" he went on.
nink," Rosie answered. "But I

didn't get a clear view of him. It all happened so quickly."

"What about you?" Officer Dale asked George.

"Well, no," said George. "I was too busy trying to hold my horse."

"And did either of you get the tag number by any chance?" he asked.

"No, I'm afraid not," Rosie said.

Rosie watched as Officer Dale scribbled one last thing down and snapped his notepad shut.

"Is that all you need to know?" Rosie asked quietly.

"For now," the policeman said in a kind voice. "If you want to get into the car, we'll give you a lift back to the stables."

Rosie and George climbed into the back. Rosie stared out of the window. She couldn't believe all this had happened – only an hour ago she had ridden so confidently out of Sandy Lane.

"Do you think you might find the driver?" she heard George asking the police, as they drove back along the winding roads.

"Hmm." Officer Dale was hesitant. "To be honest with you, we're in a very difficult position – as the car didn't actually hit anything..."

"But it was obvious the man drove too close to us," George interrupted.

"Maybe," Officer Dale went on. "But it'll be very difficult to prove, and without a tag number it's unlikely we'll be able to find him anyway."

Rosie wasn't listening to the continuing conversation. As she stared dejectedly out of the window, her mind drifted off. That car had definitely accelerated. It had been no accident. Poor Beth. As

31

‾ned into the drive off Sandy Lane,
‿irl lying crumpled on the ground
‾'s mind. She took a deep breath. What
‾v going to tell Nick and Sarah?

4

HOLDING THE FORT

"Well, it could have been worse," said Charlie. "At least all the other riders are back in one piece. And none of the horses are injured."

It was late in the day, and the Sandy Lane regulars were huddled in the tack room. It seemed as though they'd been there for hours, just trying to decide what to do. And it had been a long day. A day that had started off so promisingly and ended in disaster.

"It's as Rosie suspected," Tom said, putting down the phone from Beth's mother. "Beth's broken her leg." He took a deep breath. "They think it's going to take at least six weeks to heal, so she's not going to be around at Sandy Lane for some time. She's going to have to stay at home till she's fully recovered." Tom looked around the tack room at the gloomy faces staring back at him.

"What did her mother say we should do?" Rosie

asked. "Who's going to run Sandy Lane?"

"Don't worry, Rosie," Tom replied. "It's all in hand. I said we'd phone Nick's friend. Beth's mother was going to do it, but she seemed quite relieved when I offered instead. I suppose I'd better call him now." Tom reached for the number on the bulletin board.

"What's his name?" Rosie asked.

"Dick Bryant," Tom answered. "Shhh." Tom motioned to his lips as he dialed the number and waited patiently.

"No answer," he said finally.

"We'll have to phone Nick and Sarah," Rosie said.

"No," said Tom. "I don't want to worry Nick and Sarah if we don't have to. They've got enough to think about at the moment. We'll pack things up here, then if we can't get hold of Dick Bryant tonight, we'll try him again tomorrow."

"But what about tomorrow's lessons?" Rosie said. "Shouldn't we cancel them?"

"No... not yet," said Tom. "We'll manage. It's only for a day. I can always take over Beth's lessons and then we'll divide the rides between us."

Rosie wasn't convinced.

"Look," said Tom. "By tomorrow, we'll have gotten hold of Dick Bryant and things will be back to normal."

"Unless we don't phone Dick Bryant at all..." Charlie started.

"Oh Charlie!" Rosie exclaimed. "Not another of your crazy schemes."

"Not that crazy," he went on. "We could run Sandy Lane ourselves. It is the Spring break after all. I'm sure we could manage until Nick and Sarah get back. They'd be so pleased..."

"Don't even think about it," Tom said. "We can't possibly do that. Nick would go crazy."

"I suppose you're right," Charlie said, shrugging his shoulders. "It was just an idea. You must admit, it would be fun."

"Fun, but totally insane." Tom was irritated now. "But we can hold the fort till tomorrow evening, can't we?"

There were faint murmurings and then everyone nodded in agreement.

"OK. If that's all agreed, I can think of twelve hungry horses waiting to be fed. Let's get going."

"I'll run across to the house and lock up," said Alex. "Turn some lights on, make it look lived in... that sort of thing."

"Good idea," said Tom. "There's an extra set of keys in the drawer. Make sure you do it right. Oh and don't let's say anything about what's happened yet," Tom went on. "Not until we have everything set. You know what parents are like. They'll only worry and one of them is bound to try and get hold of Nick."

There was a quick pause as everyone exchanged nervous glances. Rosie felt uneasy. She didn't like keeping things from her parents. Still, it was only for a day and no one else seemed worried by it. She didn't want to be the odd one out.

Quickly, she followed the others outside as they began packing up the stables for the night.

* * * * * * * * * * * * * * * * *

The next morning passed uneventfully at Sandy Lane. Tom still hadn't managed to get hold of Dick Bryant. Every time he called there was no reply. At two o'clock, the regulars met in the tack room and delegated tasks for the afternoon.

"I'll take that private lesson and Rosie and Jess – do you think you could take the 2 o'clock ride out?" Tom asked.

"Of course!" said Rosie, her eyes lighting up. It was the ride that went to the lighthouse – her favorite ride. Hurriedly, she skipped to Pepper's stall.

"Did you hear that, Pepper?" she called. "We're taking a ride out this afternoon."

Pepper turned around to look at her and snorted lethargically.

"Come on, where's your energy?' she asked the little black and white pony.

"All right Rosie?" Jess's head appeared over the door.

"Fine." Rosie smiled at her friend.

"Can you tack up Blackjack?" Jess asked. "David Taylor's here and his mother wants to see him mounted for his private lesson."

"OK, I'll be there in a moment," Rosie said quickly. "Hello Mrs. Taylor," she called, hurrying over to Blackjack's stall. "I'll just get Blackjack's saddle. Tom's taking David's lesson this afternoon."

"Tom?" Mrs. Taylor looked surprised. "But where's Beth?" she asked, concerned.

"She's had an accident," said Rosie. "She was knocked off her horse by a car."

"Is she all right?" Mrs. Taylor asked.

"I'm afraid she's broken her leg," Rosie said. "And

it's going to take six weeks to mend."

"Oh dear." Mrs. Taylor was hesitant. "But is Tom capable of giving lessons?"

"Yes. He's an excellent rider, and it's only for today – some of Nick's friends are coming in to help tomorrow," Rosie said, silently praying that she wouldn't be struck down for lying. Well, it was only a little white lie. She was sure that when Tom got hold of Dick Bryant, he'd come right away

Rosie gritted her teeth as she tightened Blackjack's girth. "Come on, breathe in," she said to the little black pony. "We'll be back to normal tomorrow," Rosie went on, leading the pony out of the stall.

"Hmm," Mrs. Taylor answered. "I suppose that's all right then – if it's only for today. And you did say that Tom is a good rider..."

"The best," Rosie interrupted.

"If Nick trusts him, I'm sure it will be all right. Come on, David," she called to her son.

Rosie helped the little boy into the saddle and circled the pony around the grounds as Tom hurried over.

"Hi David," Tom called. "Are you ready?"

"Yes," the little boy answered, his eyes shining.

Rosie smiled as she watched them set off to the outdoor ring for the lesson.

"I'll be back at three to pick David up," Mrs. Taylor called, getting back into her car.

"All right Mrs. Taylor," Rosie answered. Hurriedly she made her way back to Pepper's stall and, after tacking him up, led him out to join the rest of the riders who had gathered outside for the ride.

There was a girl from the year below her at school

on Minstrel, a boy with dark hair riding Hector, a blonde girl she didn't recognize with Jester and Jess was on Storm Cloud.

"All ready?" Rosie asked the riders.

"Yes," said the blonde girl, lifting up the saddle flap to tighten the girth.

Excitedly the riders wound their way out. Jess headed the line and Rosie brought up the rear. The horses trotted down the drive and into the lane. Rosie felt the spring in Pepper's heels as they turned into the fields.

"OK. Let's have a canter," Jess called from the front. "All meet up by those trees," she pointed. Rosie waited for the other horses to set off and then, with a little nudge from her heels, she pushed Pepper on. She sat tight to the saddle. Racing forward as they headed for the trees, Rosie felt a rush of excitement run through her. There was nothing like a ride to exhilarate her.

It was a wonderful ride. At the end of the hour, the ride wound its way along Sandy Lane. As they rode back into the stables, Rosie breathed a sigh of relief – so far so good.

"How was David's lesson, Tom?" Rosie called, as she led Pepper back into his stall.

"Great," he answered, his eyes gleaming. "I really enjoyed teaching him. I never thought I'd have the patience."

Rosie couldn't help smiling. Anyone who had the patience to spend a whole summer training a horse the way Tom had Chancey, was bound to be a good teacher. Rosie looked fondly at her friend. As he turned away, Rosie crossed the grounds to check the appointment book. Pepper wasn't needed again that afternoon so she decided to do an extra good job of grooming him.

"Meeting in the tack room at five," Jess called into Pepper's stall.

"OK." Rosie smiled contentedly. Everything seemed to be going so smoothly. She wondered if Tom had gotten hold of Dick Bryant yet. Hurrying to the tack room, Pepper's saddle slung over her arm, she joined the others.

"OK everyone," said Tom. "As you know, I've been trying to get hold of Dick Bryant all day and there's still no reply, so we'll have to make a group decision here. I personally think we should wait one more day. We can cope, can't we?"

There were low murmurings and everyone exchanged uncertain glances.

"I know we agreed that if we still hadn't gotten hold of Dick Bryant this evening, we'd phone Nick and Sarah, but things have run smoothly enough haven't they?"

"Definitely," said Charlie. Slowly, the others all nodded in agreement.

"Good," said Tom. "Let's wait until tomorrow and if we haven't gotten hold of him then, we really will have to phone Nick and Sarah."

It had all been decided so quickly that Rosie hadn't even had time to feel worried about it. In fact, the thought of spending another day running Sandy Lane filled her with nervous excitement. Today had gone so well. Tomorrow could be even better. Whistling to herself, she hurried out of the tack room.

5

THE NEWCOMERS

Rosie got to the stables early the next day. It was a cold, crisp spring morning and the sun peered through the clouds. All was peaceful at Sandy Lane.

"Morning, Storm Cloud," she called as the dappled gray pony looked inquisitively from her stall.

Rosie smiled to herself as she propped up her bike and hurried over to the tack room. She groped around under the mat to find the key and unlocked the door. Taking the appointment book out of the drawer, she glanced at the rides. Three trail rides and two lessons. She could get used to running Sandy Lane. She would be disappointed when they finally reached Dick Bryant. And then a wave of guilt ran through her as she thought of the lie she had told Mrs. Taylor yesterday – that they were expecting Dick Bryant the next day.

Pushing these thoughts to the back of her mind,

she rummaged around in the desk drawer for the key to the house and crossed the yard. Nick and Sarah's black labrador, Ebony, almost knocked her over with excitement as she opened the back door.

"All right, all right," Rosie laughed. "You'll have your breakfast in a moment," she said. As she turned around, she looked out of the window and saw a tall, wiry man walking up the drive. She glanced at her watch. Seven thirty.

"Strange time to be booking a lesson, isn't it Ebony?" she said. "Well, he'll just have to wait."

Paws perched on the kitchen table, Ebony looked anxiously at his food. Rosie pulled the tin opener out of the drawer and quickly spooned the dog food into his bowl.

"Better you than me," she said, wrinkling up her nose as Ebony bounded over to his bowl.

She looked out of the window again, and this time the man was stubbing a cigarette out in the yard, grinding his foot into the ground. She felt irritated. You should never smoke near a stable, not with all the hay and straw around. Everything could so easily go up in flames.

Silently, she observed the visitor. She didn't like his looks. The muscles in his cheeks twitched and his eyes narrowed as he turned and surveyed the stables.

"Now what's he up to, Ebony?" She smiled down at the black labrador.

He seemed to be counting the stalls. What was he doing? thought Rosie. And where had he come from? He hadn't arrived by car and the first bus to Sandy Lane didn't arrive until eight.

Hurrying out of the house, she approached the

stranger.

"Can I help you?" she asked politely. The man spun around, startled.

"Whew, you made me jump," he said, looking her up and down. "I'm here to help *you* actually," he continued, smiling slowly. "I'm a friend of Nick and Sarah's."

Rosie looked puzzled.

"Nick and Sarah Brooks? You do know them, don't you?" the man went on, waiting for a response.

"Of course," said Rosie. "It's just that we weren't expecting anyone..."

"Well, Nick gave me a call yesterday," the man said, not giving Rosie a chance to finish her sentence. "He told me about Beth's accident and asked me to come along and help out. I got here as quickly as I could."

"Oh," said Rosie, looking the man up and down.

Rosie realized she had been staring and was quick to collect her manners. "So, you must be Dick Bryant then," she said.

"Dick Bryant?" Now it was the man's turn to look puzzled.

"Yes, Nick left us your number. We've been trying to get hold of you for the last two days, but there's been no answer," Rosie said.

"Oh... Dick Bryant." The man let out a low, throaty laugh. "No, I'm Sam Durant. Sorry, we haven't been formally introduced." He held out his hand. "Pleased to meet you. No, Dick's away at the moment. That's why Nick asked me to come and help out."

Rosie scratched her head, trying to make sense of it all. "So Nick knows about the accident then, does he?" she asked.

"Yes, apparently your stable girl phoned him," the man went on.

"Oh," said Rosie, anxiously. "Well, what did Nick say? Was he worried? Are they coming back?"

"Whoa, wait a minute," Sam said, holding his hand in the air. "One question at a time. Of course Nick was worried, that's why he called Vanessa and me in to help."

"Vanessa?" Rosie questioned.

"Didn't I mention my wife, Vanessa?" he answered. "She'll be coming too. Nick said we could use the house until he and Sarah get back," he said.

"Oh." Rosie's brain was working overtime. "I see," she said. "So you're coming to *live* at Sandy Lane, is that right?"

"That's about the sum of it," he went on.

"Well, I think you'd better wait and talk to Tom and the others then," she said quickly.

"Tom?" The man looked irritated. Rosie didn't really know why she was being so stubborn. There was just something about him she didn't really like; something about his silky smooth way of talking.

"I'm sure there won't be a problem, but you'd better speak to them," Rosie went on.

"Of course there won't be a problem, my dear," the man went on. "It's all been straightened out, so there's nothing to talk about, *is there*?"

He was still smiling as he held Rosie's gaze, but his words had a sinister ring to them. Rosie felt uneasy as he turned away again.

"Vanessa and I will be back at two o'clock to move in and meet the others," he called over his shoulder.

And that seemed to be the end of it. Before Rosie

could say another word, the man had turned on his heels and headed off down the drive.

"But wait!" she called desperately.

Rosie's words rang out hollowly and the man's departing frame didn't turn back to answer her call. She felt worried. It had all happened so quickly. She should have asked some more questions. She felt angry at herself, and at the awful man. Who did he think he was? Just wait till she told the others.

Rosie picked up a broom and started to sweep. The more she thought about it, the less she was able to find a real reason for disliking the man. She hated to admit it to herself, but perhaps she would have felt the same about anyone stepping in to take over the stables when they had been managing so well on their own. If Sam and his wife really were going to be running Sandy Lane, it wasn't a good idea to be on the wrong side of them. Rosie felt a little nervous at the thought of having to tell her friends what had been said. Still, she hadn't liked the man. There was just something about him...

Rosie was lost in thought when she was suddenly brought back to earth with a jolt by the sound of excited voices at the stables. She peered over the stable door. Everyone had arrived. Stepping out of the box, she tried to attract their attention.

"Listen everyone. I've got something to tell you all," Rosie started nervously. She cleared her throat as her friends gathered around and she began to recount the story of the early morning events.

As Rosie finished, there was a disappointed silence and then she was hit by a barrage of questions.

"What about Dick Bryant?"

"When are Sam and Vanessa arriving?"

"What did Nick say?"

"Were they worried?"

"When are they coming back?"

"I don't know," Rosie wailed foolishly. "I didn't manage to find all that out. All I know is that Sam's coming back at two."

"But what was he like?" Jess asked.

"Awful," Rosie said despondently.

"Why?" Tom asked. "Why was he so awful?"

"Well." Rosie was hesitant. "He just didn't look right somehow, that's all," she said, waving her hands in a flustered fashion. "I don't know. I just don't like the idea of strangers coming in and running Sandy Lane."

"Tell us the whole story again," said Tom.

So Rosie ran through the early morning events again... with a few embellishments. Then she looked around at her friends, expecting to see agreement in their faces.

"I really haven't explained things at all well, have I?" she said.

"Perhaps we should phone Nick and Sarah in Kentucky," Jess started.

"Look, I think it's only fair to give Sam and Vanessa a few days to settle in first," Tom interrupted. "I know I sound boring and grown-up, but it's a big thing, running the stable. We don't want to do anything to mess it up for Nick and Sarah, do we? And if Nick has sent Sam in to help, well we can't just send him away saying Rosie doesn't like him."

"Tom's right, Rosie," said Jess. "Let's wait a while.

"Yes... maybe they are awful, but we have to put

up with them," Charlie said grudgingly.

"And let's try and get everything looking spick-and-span around the stable," Kate added, "after all, if they're going to be reporting back to Nick and Sarah, we want them to say we've done a good job."

"OK," Rosie said uncertainly. "You don't think I was going overboard?" she asked Jess as they headed to the stalls. "Sort of rude?"

"Of course not," said Jess, trying to reassure her friend. "We don't want Sam coming in here and thinking he can totally rearrange things, do we? Not now that things are going so well."

"No, we don't," said Rosie, encouraged by her friend's faith in her. "You're right," she went on. "Come on, let's start mucking out the stalls."

Jess and Rosie hurried off in different directions. By eight thirty, twelve stalls had been mucked out, and the horses all groomed and fed.

"When's the first lesson of the day?" Jess called, as she entered the tack room.

"Nine o'clock," Rosie answered. "Tom's giving a private lesson and you and I are taking out the trail ride."

"Good," said Jess. "I want to get out. I feel as though I've been mucking out all morning."

* * * * * * * * * * * * * * * * *

Two o'clock came and went. By three, there was still no sign of Sam and Vanessa.

"Come on," said Tom. "It's no good sitting around tapping our fingers. The 3 o'clock ride's waiting to go out."

"OK," said Rosie.

It wasn't until five fifteen that a white Suburban pulled up in the yard. A motley assortment of Sandy Lane heads – horses and all – popped over the stall doors to see the new arrivals at the stables.

Sam Durant jumped out of the car, followed by a stylish woman in her early thirties. Clad in a beautiful pair of designer black britches, a glossy silk scarf wrapped around her neck, she peered out from behind a pair of dark sunglasses. Her long blonde hair was tied back in a sleek French braid.

"They're not how I imagined them, Rosie," Tom whispered, obviously impressed.

"Why? What did you expect?" Rosie muttered back.

"Something less elegant I suppose."

Rosie felt embarrassed. "They hardly look very horsy though, do they?" she grumbled.

"I don't know," Jess interrupted. "Horsy people don't have to be scruffy. They look important."

Now the man was striding over to Tom and holding out his hand.

"I take it you must be Tom," he said grandly. "I've heard all about you from Nick... said you were quite the little rider. I'm Sam Durant. You may have heard of me from my days as an eventer," he said.

"Yes, yes," said Tom, blushing with pride at the words of praise from an obvious expert.

Rosie shrugged her shoulders. She had never heard

the name Sam Durant before and felt very ill at ease with what she was hearing. Tom actually seemed to have warmed to Sam, and now all of her friends had gathered around.

"And this is my wife, Vanessa," Sam continued, introducing the woman beside him.

Rosie looked on, silently watching, as her friends eagerly introduced themselves. Rosie stood back from the group and frowned. She couldn't go back on what she had said about Sam now. She had to stick to her guns.

"OK," said Sam turning to the group. "You seem to have been managing things just fine here. How have you been going about it all?"

"We've each been responsible for looking after two horses and then we take turns leading rides," Tom explained. "And I've been taking over Beth's lessons for the last couple of days," he went on hesitantly. "I know I shouldn't have really but..."

"Perfect," Sam said. "We could continue in the same way then. We'll share giving lessons. You can do the ones in the morning, and I'll do the ones in the afternoon."

Tom beamed. Rosie couldn't believe what she was hearing.

"But Tom, you're not really qualified to give lessons are you?" she whispered.

"Rosie," Tom hissed. "If Sam thinks I'm up to it, then I'm up to it." He turned around to smile at Sam.

"Right... all settled?" Sam went on. "I'm happy with that."

"I bet you are," Rosie said under her breath. "All the less work for you."

"Vanessa can arrange the rides, and all those sorts of things," Sam said now. "I don't want it to look as though we're completely taking over." He flashed them a smile.

"And what about our Tentenden training sessions?" Jess asked anxiously.

"Are you entered for the Tentenden Team Chase?" Sam asked.

"Yes," Jess said. "Nick has already picked the four of us to represent Sandy Lane." She indicated herself, Tom, Charlie and Rosie. "And we've set up a schedule of training sessions."

"Good. I'll take over those sessions then, if you want me to," said Sam.

"That sounds great," Tom enthused.

"OK," Sam said, taking the keys to the house that Tom was holding out. "That's all agreed then. We'll be settling in if anyone wants us," he added. Vanessa gave them a regal wave. She hadn't said a thing.

"Well, at least that's the last of them for today," Rosie muttered under her breath, as the couple slipped off to the house.

"Don't be like that Rosie," said Kate crossly. "Why are you being so funny about them? They're nice."

"Hmm. A little too nice," Rosie said gruffly.

"Look, I don't know why you've taken this instant dislike to them," said Tom. "It sounds like they're not going to bother us too much. They'll leave us to do pretty much as we like and help with Tentenden too. It's perfect."

"But there's something not quite right about them," Rosie mused.

"You've been reading too many detective stories,

Rosie," Tom teased. "We're going to have to start calling you the Sandy Lane Super Sleuth if you're not careful." Rosie looked hurt.

"I'm only joking," he said, giving her arm a little squeeze.

"I know," said Rosie, following the others into the tack room. "And I suppose I did make a mistake over Nick and Sarah closing down Sandy Lane too."

That was it. She was being silly. Things would be all right in the morning, she was sure of it. She mustn't be so quick to judge people. Everyone else had liked Sam and Vanessa.

Settling down on the floor, she picked up a piece of saddle soap, and began cleaning the tack. An uncomfortable silence pervaded the room. She looked at her watch. Six thirty, and she'd said she would be home at seven for supper. She'd have to leave in ten minutes. Rosie's thoughts were interrupted as the phone in the tack room started ringing and Tom got up to answer it. It was Beth's mother.

"Yes Mrs. Wilson," Tom was saying. "We're fine... no, we didn't get hold of Dick Bryant, but it's all right. Nick and Sarah have sent some friends in to run the stables – Sam and Vanessa Durant... yes they're great. Tell Beth to hurry up and get better. We'll be over to visit her soon... yes that's fine."

Rosie looked at her watch. She'd have to hurry. Getting up from the floor, she crossed the room to the door. Everyone was tuned into the telephone conversation, carefully listening to what Tom was saying.

"Bye everyone," she called forlornly. "I'm going home now." But no one answered her. Rosie shrugged her shoulders and slipped out of the doorway, heading over to her bicycle. For the first time ever, Rosie felt like an outsider at Sandy Lane. Sadly, she turned her bicycle out of the yard, taking one quick glance behind her at the tack room, now lit up by a yellow glow, the laughter spilling out into the night.

6

STANDARDS SLIP

In the excitement following the arrival of the newcomers to Sandy Lane, the forthcoming Tentenden Team Chase seemed to have been forgotten. The Sandy Lane regulars found themselves extremely busy. There was so much to do – so many rides to organize, so many lessons to give, that they hardly had time to fit in any training. Four days had passed and Sam had only taken them out over the cross-country course once.

"Where's Sam?" Rosie called, hurrying over to Alex and Tom. "I've been banging on the door of the house all morning. I'm sure he's inside, but there's no answer."

"But that was part of the deal, wasn't it?" Tom returned quickly. "I give lessons in the morning, he gives lessons in the afternoon and we all help around the stables. He doesn't need to be around all the time."

Rosie raised her eyebrows.

"They don't seem to be helping much around the stables though, do they?" she said gruffly.

"Oh Rosie. You're not still going on about that are you?" Tom said crossly. "Come on. Give them a chance. And Sam's excellent over cross-country."

"He may be very experienced," Rosie said hesitantly. "But personally I don't think I'm learning a great deal. He's too busy congratulating himself most of the time. Anyway, it's the stables I'm worried about, not his riding skills," she continued. "The earnings have been down for the last three days in a row and Vanessa's completely useless. It was better when we did the appointment book ourselves. Yesterday, there were *two* double bookings. Nick and Sarah never turn pupils away, especially not regulars like Melissa White. And Melissa said that she might even try out the Clarendon Equestrian Center. It's the last thing Nick and Sarah need – having another stables' earnings boosted because of us."

"It was a mistake, Rosie," Tom said tersely. "Accidents do happen. Melissa wouldn't really go to the Clarendon Equestrian Center. It's only been open six months and it's already got a bad reputation. The horses look all right, but they're really badly schooled. And as for the owner, Ralph Winterson, he's never there anyway. He just leaves the stable girls to do everything."

"He's been cited for cruelty to horses before too, Rosie," Alex added. "And I heard a rumor going around that he had to close down his last stables for cruelty to animals. He only got away with it because it was his word against a little girl's. But no one doubted for a moment that he'd been sedating the horses."

"Whatever you say," Rosie said crossly. "But I do still need to see Sam... and now rather than next year. He needs to sign the Tentenden entry form," she went on. "If it doesn't go today it'll miss the closing date. I'm almost tempted to forge his signature."

Rosie wandered away, trying to look as if she didn't care. But deep down she did care. She minded very much what her friends thought of her. She would have to keep quiet from now on; even Jess had started telling her to give it a rest.

Rosie hurried into the tack room to finish off the entry form. Methodically, she filled in the gaps in her neat, sloping handwriting, chewing the end of her pen as she carefully read the form. It was only when Jess put her head around the door that she realized how long she had spent poring over it.

"Look Rosie," Jess cried excitedly. "A postcard from Nick and Sarah."

"Read it out then," said Rosie, taking the pen out of her mouth.

"Dear all," Jess started. "Arrived safely. Sarah's dad is on the road to recovery, so all is well. Hope Beth is working you hard for Tentenden. Very busy out here, but should still be back on the 20th as planned. Tell you more about it when we see you. Love Nick and Sarah."

"It looks like they must have sent it before Beth's accident," said Rosie, thinking aloud.

"I suppose so," Jess said, "I can't really read the postmark. I'll pin it to the bulletin board where the others can see it. Come on, Rosie," she added.

"Pepper's waiting for you. And Sam has said he'll take us all over the cross-country course."

"Cross-country?" Rosie said puzzled. "I didn't know we had training this morning. Is Sam up and about then?"

"Yes and waiting," Jess grinned. "And he says he'll take Kate and Alex too, not just the team for Tentenden."

"Oh," said Rosie, shrugging her shoulders. Jumping to her feet, she left the application form spread out on the desk in front of her. It could wait another hour. She followed Jess out of the tack room, just as Tom led Whispering Silver out of her stall.

"Where are you going with Whisp, Tom?" Rosie called out.

"Sam wants to try her over the cross-country," Tom answered quickly.

"What? But Nick doesn't let *anyone* ride Whisp over the course," said Rosie. "Not even him. Her legs aren't up to it, not if she takes a heavy knock. She's getting older now. Nick wants to be careful with her."

"Sam thinks it'll strengthen her legs if he gives her some good exercise, and he's going to jump her carefully, Rosie," Tom said shortly. "Why are you always questioning his judgement? He is here with Nick's approval you know. And I'm sure he knows better than any of us what her legs can and can't take. He's been riding for years."

Rosie shrugged her shoulders and turned away. Tom had surely put her in her place. She wanted to say something to Sam, to question his decision to ride Whispering Silver, but somehow she didn't. Leading Pepper out to join the others, she shivered as a gust of wind blew across the grounds.

"Is everyone here?" Sam asked, opening the gate to the fields at the back. Rosie followed on after the others in a daze.

"Everyone gather over by the big beech tree," Sam continued.

The horses trotted over to the tree and stopped in a group. Sam cantered over to join them.

"OK. Let's get going. And remember, speed is the key."

Rosie felt a nervous tremor run through her. She knew that speed was vital but it wasn't her greatest skill. Surely care and safety were as important too? She had never been intimidated by the cross-country course before, never doubted her own ability. But suddenly she felt unsure. Was it just a week and a half ago that she had stood so confidently in front of the jumps? Suddenly the tiger trap seemed to tower above her and the other fences loomed dangerously in the distance.

"I'll go around once to show you how it's done," Sam said brusquely, snapping Rosie out of her trance. "And then, when I'm back, I'll watch you one by one. OK? And by the way everyone, I'm not sure about the choice for the Tentenden team," he laughed, looking at Rosie. "So convince me with your riding."

Rosie gulped. Sam couldn't alter the team now, could he? She looked around at the animated faces of her friends. None of them seemed worried by Sam's remarks. She opened her mouth to protest, and closed it again. Digging her nails into her hands to stop the tears, she turned to Jess.

"Did you hear what Sam said? He wants me out of

the team."

"Don't be silly, Rosie," said Jess laughing. "It wasn't aimed at you. I'm sure Sam wouldn't alter the team now... not after all the training we've put in. It's just his way of keeping us on our toes."

"I hope you're right," Rosie said despondently. She didn't know what to think. Maybe she was overreacting but it certainly hadn't seemed that way to her. She felt faint as she turned to look at the course.

Staring into the distance, Rosie watched Sam turn Whispering Silver toward the first fence with a crack from his whip. The horse stumbled and hurtled toward the tiger trap at breakneck speed as Sam crouched low onto her neck, his legs tucked neatly beneath him. They rocketed over the jump and, as they landed, Sam pushed her on. Faster and faster Whisp raced. Rosie could hardly bear to watch as the horse was spurred forward. Whisp responded bravely and battled her way over the next jump and then they went out of sight and into the woods.

"Wow. They're going fast," Jess cried, her eyes glinting brightly. "Are you all right there, Rosie?" she asked turning in the saddle and seeing her friend's white face.

"Yes," Rosie breathed.

But Rosie felt sick. She wasn't impressed. She knew Sam was asking too much of Whisp. Nervously she bit her lip, training her eyes on the outline of horse and rider. Nick would die if anything happened to that horse. Rosie dreaded to think what was going on.

"Here they are now," Tom cried, as the pair of them emerged from the trees and headed for the next jump. Horse and rider skimmed over the fence and plunged into the water. But Whisp was sinking, her legs thrashing around under her as she tried to gather momentum. Tired, she staggered up the bank.

Rosie held her breath as they rode over the zigzag rails and then the gate, onto the stone wall. The ground fell away as horse and rider galloped up the hill and neared the group. Rosie grimaced. Whispering Silver was in a lather, her body was bathed in sweat as she quivered in the wind. Sam's britches, clean that morning, were splattered with mud.

"That was fast, Sam. It looked amazing," Tom gasped.

"It was," Sam said nonchalantly. "Now you try. I must say, I did have some trouble in the woods. I think the old horse was tiring, took a bit of a beating."

Rosie trembled. Her heart felt heavy as she looked down at Whispering Silver's delicate legs. Sam's words echoed in her head as Tom galloped Chancey to the first fence and Sam clicked his stopwatch.

Rosie had never seen them go so fast. They were out of control. And she knew Chancey wasn't fit enough for it. It could strain his heart. But Tom must know what he was doing – Chancey was his horse after all. Thundering over the tiger trap, they raced to the brush hurdle. Rosie could hear the sound of hooves pulsating in her ears, the sound of metal shoes striking timber as the jumps were cleared in easy succession. Chancey hardly seemed to touch the ground as he came out of the woods and approached the water jump. But no sooner was he over it and out of the water, than Tom was pressing him on to the zigzag rails. Chancey tore over them, straining at the bit as he surged on to the low gate.

Sam clicked his stop watch as they cleared the stone wall.

"Good." He beamed as Tom returned to the group.

Good! Rosie couldn't believe her ears. It had been bordering on dangerous. And, as she had volunteered to go last, she would have to watch another four of her friends ride crazily around the course before it was even her turn.

She turned Pepper away from the group, trying to keep her cool. She tried to relax as she loosened him up, but all she could hear were the words 'speed, speed, speed,' ringing in her ears. She knew she wasn't going to have a good round... knew that by going fast, she would jeopardize her style. She couldn't bring herself to watch the others. When eventually it was her turn to ride the course, she had no idea how they had done. She circled Pepper, waiting for Sam to indicate that she should start, watching him for a flicker of movement. Then Sam nodded his head and she nudged the little pony forward. She turned him to the start and pushed him on into a canter.

"Faster."

Rosie heard the roar from behind her and tried to lengthen Pepper's stride. Pepper tried to put in an extra stride as he headed for the tiger trap and stumbled over the fence. Rosie knew she had completely misdirected the little pony. Her arms and legs were all over the place as she tugged at Pepper's reins in an effort to slow him down. Hurtling over the brush hurdle, they bounded on to the hayrack.

Pepper was excited now and he snorted impatiently. Rolling his eyes, enthralled by the speed, he surged ahead and for the next two jumps, Rosie found herself hanging behind. They thundered into the woods.

Rosie felt the panic rising in her throat as the low-hanging branches brushed against her clothes. She was slipping in the saddle. She didn't know how she managed to stay on over the tires. And when the little pony checked himself at the water jump, Rosie almost flew over his head. Splashing on through the water, Rosie lost a stirrup. Desperately trying to regain her seat, she found herself completely off-balance for the next two fences and was shaking when she joined the rest of the group. It had been a terrible round.

"Not bad," said Sam, clicking his stop watch.

Rosie stopped for a minute to catch her breath. Her heart was pounding and her arms ached. She had been frightened, actually frightened. Everyone must have seen that.

"Good pace, Rosie," said Jess. "If we all go that speed at Tentenden, we might have a chance of winning."

Rosie didn't know what to say to her friend. She turned away, disgusted with herself. Hadn't Jess seen how badly she had ridden? Nothing had been said about her place on the team and her time was still the third fastest. But she didn't feel happy with the way she had ridden.

Turning back to the stables, Rosie led Pepper back into his stall. She tied him to the ring and closed the door behind her. Relieved to be alone at last, she untacked the pony.

"I won't let Sam spoil Tentenden for us, Pepper," she whispered to the little horse. As soon as she'd finished sponging him off, she went off to complete the Tentenden application.

Adding the last finishing touches to the form, Rosie fished out a stamp from her pocket and attached it to the envelope. Then she hurried to find Sam. Knocking at the door of the house, she waited patiently.

"Sam," Rosie said hesitantly as he answered the door. "I've got the entry form for Tentenden here. Do you think you could sign it before I mail it? It should really go off today to make sure it gets there on Friday."

"Just leave it there Rosie. I'll sign it and send it myself," Sam said.

But he wouldn't meet her eyes and Rosie felt uneasy. Sam hadn't said anything more about a change of team, but Rosie didn't trust him a bit. Would he actually leave her name on the form, or would he substitute someone else's? She hesitated. She couldn't bring herself to ask him. She just wasn't sure she wanted to hear the answer.

7

FROM BAD TO WORSE

Sleep didn't come easily to Rosie that night and when it did, it was disturbed by dreams... dreams of horses falling into open ditches and thrashing around in icy water. Tossing and turning, she woke in a cold sweat. She looked at her watch. Six o'clock. There wasn't any point in trying to get back to sleep. She'd have to be up in half an hour anyway.

Drawing back the curtains, she looked out of the window and sighed. It was just getting light and an eerie mist hung over the fields. Rosie felt uneasy as she remembered yesterday's events. Sam really shouldn't have given Whisp such a hard ride. She hoped the horse would be all right. As for her riding, it had been appalling.

Reaching to her bedside chair, she grabbed her clothes and pulled them under her comforter. They were cold to the touch as she struggled to put them on.

On the count of three, Rosie threw back the covers and jumped out of bed. Picking up her waterproof jacket, she tiptoed down the stairs and grabbed a piece of bread from the kitchen before making her way outside to her bike. The air felt heavy with rain. All was still and silent as she cycled to Sandy Lane. She passed no one on the empty country roads.

Turning into the drive, she rode into the yard and hopped off her bike, propping it up against the water trough as she walked over to Whisp's stall.

At first Rosie couldn't see anything when she looked over the door, but once her eyes had grown accustomed to the dark, she could see the shape of the horse lying down on the floor. Whisp looked up and struggled to her feet. Rosie grimaced as she realized that one of the horse's back legs was swollen. Whisp's head hung low and she balanced painfully on three legs.

"Damn you, Sam," Rosie muttered through gritted teeth.

Drawing back the bolt on the door, she entered the stall, talking sweetly to the horse all the time.

"It's OK Whisp. You're going to be all right, poor old lady," she crooned. Whisp turned her face toward her and snickered softly. Swiftly, Rosie ran her hand down the horse's leg and felt the heat.

"I think we'll have to have the vet called out for you," she said, fondly patting the gray neck.

Rosie hurried over to the tack room and dialed the vet's number. When he heard what was wrong, he promised to come right away. For the moment, there was nothing more Rosie could do, so she waited anxiously by the gate.

Soon the others arrived at Sandy Lane. Rosie was gloomy as she told them what had happened.

"Oh," said Tom sheepishly. "Poor Whisp. Sam did take her around pretty fast. I suppose we'd better cancel her rides."

Rosie headed off to check the bookings. Slipping into the tack room, she opened up the appointment book. That was strange – today's page seemed to have been torn out. Rosie flicked through the book. Even stranger – all the other days were there, but today's was clearly missing.

"Tom," she called. "Tom, do you know anything about this?"

Tom hurried into the tack room as Rosie held up the book with the ripped page.

"Where can it have gone?" he puzzled. "Who can have taken that page? It's our only record of who's riding who. How will we ever figure it out? Can you remember?"

"Not really. I know that Melissa White's on Pepper at some time but that's about it. Vanessa's the only person who might know," she said.

"What might I know?" a voice called.

Rosie saw Vanessa leaning in the doorway of the tack room.

"Something about this?" Tom held up the diary. "Today's page is missing. It's been torn out."

"Maybe someone tore it out by mistake," she said, looking away a little too quickly.

"Well, we need to try and figure out the bookings pretty fast," Rosie said frostily, "or we won't be ready for the day."

"Let me see," said Vanessa. "I might be able to remember. Give me ten minutes. I'll sit down and try to put a list together. Yes, I think I'll be able to do it."

"Great," said Tom. "And that must be the vet now," he said as a car pulled up in the yard.

"The vet? What's going on?" Vanessa asked.

"Don't you know Whisp is lame?" Rosie bridled, angrily striding off to meet the vet before Vanessa had a chance to answer. Tom hurried over to join her.

"Where's the patient?" the vet asked in a friendly voice.

"In here," said Tom, drawing back the bolt to Whisp's stall.

The two friends poked their heads anxiously over the stall door as the vet looked at Whisp's leg.

"Poor old lady. She's taken a knock. There's a small cut above the fetlock. It's nothing serious, but she needs to rest." He patted her neck. "I'll bandage it up," he said, setting to work. "And I'll leave you some gauze bandages to keep it clean. Make sure she isn't ridden," he said. And, as quickly as he had arrived, the vet put his car into reverse and backed out of the drive.

"Here we are," said Vanessa stepping out of the tack room and waving a piece of paper. "All straightened out?"

"As straightened out as it can be for the moment anyway. Whisp is lame and she can't be ridden – another cost the stable could have done without," Rosie muttered. "But apart from that, things are just fine," she said sarcastically.

Vanessa smiled, seemingly ignoring Rosie's words. "Well, I've put a list together," she went on. "It's all rides today and no lessons, so you should be all right."

"*We* should be all right?" Tom asked questioningly.

"Didn't Sam tell you he was away today? He's got things to straighten out. And I'm off shopping," said Vanessa. "I can trust you two to look after the stables though, can't I?"

"Sure," Tom sighed, giving the list a cursory glance before handing it on to Rosie. Rosie glanced down the names. It was a lot of work. She shrugged her shoulders. Storm Cloud, Feather, Napoleon and Minstrel had to be ready in a quarter of an hour for the ten o'clock ride for experienced riders.

"Are you listening everyone?" Rosie called as Vanessa drove out of the yard. "We don't have much time – fifteen minutes to get four horses ready – so let's make it snappy."

By two minutes to ten, the four horses were tacked up and waiting, eager and ready for the ride.

Ten o'clock came and no one arrived. They waited and waited. After all, people were sometimes late. But by ten thirty there was still no sign of anyone. Rosie was fuming.

At eleven o'clock the riders eventually turned up for their ride. Rosie's heart sank when she saw them. They were all novices, and none of the ponies waiting were novice mounts.

"Is Blackjack ready?" Mrs. Taylor asked, surprised to see Jess lead Storm Cloud out from her stall for David to ride.

"Er, I'm afraid we're a little behind this morning," said Rosie, playing for time. "We had a little accident. Whisp's lame and there seems to be a bit of a mix-up with mounts."

"Not another double booking!" Mrs. Taylor groaned. "This is getting ridiculous. Where's Sam this morning? Does he know how often this keeps on happening?"

"I should think so – he is to blame for it,' Rosie muttered through gritted teeth. She turned back to Mrs. Taylor.

"If you could give us another five minutes," she said, smiling sweetly. "We're almost there."

The regulars converged in the tack room and quickly decided what to do. Breathlessly, Jess led the unwanted ponies back to their stalls while the others hurried to get the novice mounts ready.

Rosie hurried off to Blackjack's stall. There wasn't enough time to give him a thorough grooming – a quick going-over would have to do. Hurrying to collect his saddle, she was puzzled to find it wasn't in its correct place.

"Tom, have you seen Blackjack's saddle?" she called across the yard.

"No," said Tom, swooping into the tack room and picking up Horace's tack.

"Jess, am I being stupid or something?" Rosie said turning to her friend. "I can't find Blackjack's saddle anywhere. It's not on his rack."

The two friends hunted high and low, but it was nowhere to be found.

"What are we going to do?" said Rosie. "We can't put Blackjack in another saddle. It'll rub him raw with his hollow back. That saddle was made especially for him. It cost a fortune. Nick will go nuts if it's lost."

"It's got to be here somewhere," said Jess. "A saddle can't get misplaced!"

"Come on you two. What are you up to?" Tom called into the tack room.

"Blackjack's saddle has disappeared," Jess cried.

"It couldn't have," Tom said. "It was there yesterday. It couldn't have vanished."

"Well it has," said Rosie. "David will have to ride Horace. Who's going to be the one to break the news to his mother?"

"I will," Tom groaned, when no one answered.

Swiftly crossing the yard, he tried to explain things.

"I'm really sorry, Mrs. Taylor, but I'm afraid that Blackjack's saddle is missing. If David wouldn't mind, he'll be riding Horace."

"Where's Blackjack?" the little boy wailed. "I always ride Blackjack. Where is he?" he cried. "I want to ride Blackjack!"

"I'm sorry," his mother apologized. "But David only has one riding lesson a week and he looks forward to it so much. He adores that pony."

"I do understand," said Tom sympathetically, as Mrs. Taylor led David to the car. Tom was glad when they were gone. David's mother had been very understanding, but Tom knew it was terribly unprofessional. She had every right to complain.

Things got no better as the day progressed. Vanessa's list turned out to be worse than no list at all. There were mix-ups everywhere. Pupils booked for private lessons were down for trail rides, horses had been double-booked, rides had been mysteriously canceled. The day ended up a series of disasters. As the last ride drew to a close and the horses were bolted into their stalls with their evening feeds, Rosie breathed a sigh of relief. She hoped she would never have another day like it.

Despondently, the Sandy Lane friends met in the tack room. They still hadn't found Blackjack's saddle. If it didn't turn up by the morning, they'd have to order another one. They couldn't have him missing lessons.

They counted their earnings, which were lower than usual for the third day in a row. Rosie didn't like to voice her doubts, but the sooner Nick and Sarah got back the better, as far as she was concerned.

* * * * * * * * * * * * * * * * *

Three days had passed since the dreadful ride over the cross-country course before Rosie finally plucked up enough courage to call the Tentenden office. She wanted to find out which riders Sam had actually entered on the team. He couldn't drop her now, could he? Phoning from the tack room, she felt strangely nervous.

"Hello... yes... er... I wonder if you can help me," she said nervously, as she put her money into the pay phone.

"I hope so," a voice answered.

Rosie swallowed hard. "I just wanted to check the names on the entry form for Sandy Lane Stables."

"Sure, hang on a minute," the voice at the other end answered.

Rosie waited patiently, shifting her weight from one foot to the other. The phone was eating her change. It seemed like ages before the voice returned.

"What was the name again?" asked the voice.

"Sandy Lane." Rosie took a deep breath.

"I'm afraid I don't seem to have an entry for that name."

"What?" Rosie gulped. "Are you sure?"

"Positive," the voice answered quickly. "There's nothing here under Sandy Lane. I've gone through them all."

"But the form was mailed three days ago. It should be with you by now."

"Well I don't have it."

"But what can we do?" Rosie said quietly.

"There's not a lot you can do," the voice answered sympathetically. "I'm sorry, but I'm afraid it's too late to send in another one. You'll just have to apply earlier next year."

As Rosie put the phone down, her head was swimming. She had to sit down for a few moments for it all to sink in. What had happened? Was it lost in the mail? Or... a dreadful thought dawned on Rosie. Maybe Sam hadn't mailed it after all.

Disappointment turned to rage. What had he done with it? No Tentenden Team Chase for any of them this year! Well, Sam couldn't wiggle out of this one that easily.

Rushing out of the tack room, she called all of her friends over.

"You're never going to believe this," she spluttered. "Who do you think I just spoke to?"

Everyone looked blankly at her.

"The Tentenden Office, that's who. And they don't have any record of our entry," Rosie shouted. "They say they've never received it," she said triumphantly. "And now we can't enter. It's too late."

"What?" Tom jumped to his feet. "There must be some kind of mistake."

"The only mistake was letting Sam mail the entry form for us!" Rosie snapped.

"I think we'd better go and find Sam," Tom said getting up quietly. "See what he has to say. Come on everyone."

The team trooped out of the tack room and hurried over to the house. Four faces waited for Sam to appear as Tom knocked on the back door.

"Hello, well it's the whole team," Sam said, smiling as he came to the door. "What do you want?"

Rosie stepped to the front of her friends and, before Tom could stop her, the words had spilled out in full torrent.

"You never sent it did you?" she shouted angrily. "The Tentenden form... they've never received it. All you had to do was mail it. I'm going to phone Nick," she yelled, her voice getting louder and louder.

"Now, hold on a minute, Rosie," said Sam. "What are you talking about? Of course I mailed the form," he said smoothly. "Do you mean to say they haven't received it? Look I'll give them a call now and clear things up," he said in a charming voice. "I'll be with you in a minute."

"Rosie, what do you think you're doing?" Tom said angrily, as Sam walked back into the house. "You can't go around making accusations till we find out more. You must calm down."

Rosie didn't answer him.

Impatiently, everyone stood around waiting until,

moments later, Sam appeared.

"It seems Rosie's right," he said. "They never received the form. It must have gotten lost in the mail. I explained the situation and said how hard we'd all been working, but they've already set up starting times. They just wouldn't listen. I'm sorry. I thought I'd be able to pull a few strings."

Rosie's face was black as thunder as she listened to Sam's words. Before he had a chance to finish, she had turned on her heels and was striding off toward Pepper's stall. Tom hurried to catch up with her.

"*Lost in the mail* – what a lie," she muttered, angrily. "All he had to do was put it in a mailbox and he couldn't even manage that."

"Look Rosie, we're all disappointed," Tom said, grabbing her arm. "But I'm sure Sam wouldn't say he'd mailed the form if he hadn't."

"Why not?" Rosie shrugged Tom off angrily. "How do we know what lies he's been telling to cover his mistakes. They're useless... so inefficient. We've got to phone Nick and Sarah and tell them what a mess things are in here. School starts on Monday – Sam and Vanessa won't even have us to help them then. Nick and Sarah might not even have a Sandy Lane to come back to if we leave it any longer!"

"Oh come on," said Tom, trying to get her to listen to him as she stomped across the gravel. "Aren't you just being a little over-dramatic?"

"No," said Rosie determinedly. "I don't care what you say. My mind's made up. I'm phoning them. *You* may not care, but I'd set my heart on Tentenden."

"We'd all set our hearts on Tentenden, Rosie, but if we're not entered, there's nothing we can do about it," Tom snapped. "I'm going to leave for home in a minute. Have you nearly finished here?"

"Yes," Rosie said, her jaw jutting out defiantly. "I'll just go around the stables once more and then I'm going home. See you tomorrow Tom."

"See you tomorrow," he answered, shrugging his shoulders as he walked over to his bike.

All was quiet as Tom rode out of the yard. Rosie felt a shiver run down her spine. It was creepy at the stables when there was no one else around. Shadows lurked everywhere. She must get Nick and Sarah's phone number from the bulletin board before she went home. Groping along the wall in the inky blackness of the tack room, she fumbled for the light switch.

It was very dark. Something brushed against her legs. She screamed as she flicked on the light switch to find Ebony looking up at her reproachfully.

"Silly dog," she said breathing a sigh of relief. "I thought you were someone else."

Leaning across to the bulletin board, she felt around for the scrap of paper... taxi cards, old farriers' bills, a raffle ticket. It must be here somewhere. She'd seen it only yesterday. Pulling aside each of the pieces of paper, she started to panic. Where was it? She checked the floor, the desk, the appointment book. Her heart skipped a beat. It wasn't there. It had gone. There was no doubting it, Nick and Sarah's number had disappeared. It had vanished into thin air!

8

STARTLING NEWS

Rosie's head was still reeling from shock when she got home that evening. Someone must have removed that piece of paper. Someone who didn't want her phoning Nick and Sarah and telling them about all the mishaps at Sandy Lane. And Rosie could only think of one person who that might be... Sam!

She wanted to phone Tom immediately and tell him about the missing number but she couldn't bring herself to pick up the receiver – not when he already thought she was overreacting anyway. What could she do? Rosie thought carefully. There was only one other person who might know the number... Beth. After all, Beth had phoned Nick and Sarah after her accident.

Rosie made a mental note to call her for the number in the morning. Rosie started to feel a whole lot better once she had made up her mind what to do. All right, so they had decided not to bother Nick and Sarah. But this was different. Sandy Lane was going downhill, and if she didn't do something about it, no one else would. It was only as Rosie undressed for bed that she realized how tired she was. She had been working so hard at the stables, that she had no difficulty in falling asleep that night.

When she awoke the next morning and looked at her bedside clock, she realized she had been asleep for ages. It was eight thirty. *Eight thirty.* She'd slept for ten solid hours. All thoughts of phoning Beth went out of her mind as she hurried to get to the stables.

"Mom, Mom," she cried. "I'm late. Could you give me a lift to the stables? Please? Just this once?"

"I gave you a lift last week, Rosie," Mrs. Edwards groaned. "I don't want to make a habit of it... oh, OK," she sighed, seeing Rosie's despondent face. "Grab your things. I've got to go into Colcott anyway. I'll drop you off on the way."

Rosie waited patiently by the door, willing her mother to hurry up. At last Mrs. Edwards was ready. Rosie felt subdued as she fastened her seat belt and gazed out of the window at the passing traffic. Her mother seemed to realize she didn't want to talk, and the journey passed silently.

"Thanks Mom." Rosie smiled weakly as she jumped out of the car at the bottom of Sandy Lane and walked up the drive. As she reached the corner of the stables, she was surprised to see everyone gathered in a group around Sam who was reading aloud from a piece of paper. Rosie just caught the end of what he was saying and the words made her unable to move.

"...so please go ahead and sell Pepper for me."

Rosie approached the group.

"What's going on?" she said coldly, her heart beating faster as she saw Kate's tear-stained face.

"Rosie. It's too awful for words," Kate burst out.

"Nick's selling Pepper. Sam got the letter this morning. Sandy Lane desperately needs the money and someone's offered a good price for him," Kate wailed.

"What!" Rosie cried. She heard the words screaming in her head – *But he can't, he wouldn't, not Pepper.* Instead, she found herself answering in a calm and reasonable manner.

"That can't be right. Nick would never sell Pepper," she said. "He was one of their first ponies."

"It's true, Rosie," said Tom. "They have to. Nick and Sarah need the money. I can't quite believe it myself but..."

"But Nick doesn't care about money," Rosie interrupted coldly.

"No," said Tom softly, handing her the letter. "Not normally, but Sandy Lane hasn't been doing too well lately, and there are vet bills and feed bills to pay, and then there's all the extra expenses like the flight tickets. Not forgetting that Blackjack's saddle alone is going to cost two weeks' earnings. It's all there in the letter."

"When's he going then?" Rosie asked woodenly.

"Next Friday," Sam interrupted.

"Next Friday." Rosie repeated the words quietly. "But that's so soon."

Rosie turned away clutching the letter. She felt a lump rising in her throat, almost choking her. Nick had tried to justify his reasons, explained about the endless bills, the reduced earnings, Blackjack's saddle. The list went on and on. It was all very fair, but as

Rosie read it over and over, the words seemed to get fainter and fainter. It all seemed so unreal.

"Well, work as usual," Tom said. "Try not to think about it everyone."

But as Rosie made her way over to Pepper's stall, she knew she couldn't possibly not think about it. No more Pepper...

"It seems you're going away next week Pepper," she said, opening the door to his stall. "I know that you'll miss Sandy Lane, but you'll have a new owner who'll love you enormously, and your very own paddock and orchards full of apples to look out onto and... and..." The words choked in Rosie's throat and her lips quivered as she fought back the tears. She had to stop herself. Anyone would think Pepper was her own pony the way she was acting.

"I'm going to give you a good grooming, let everyone see how beautiful you are. Come on."

Rosie tried to put it out of her mind and, picking up a body brush, she began to groom Pepper's coat until he shone.

Putting on a brave face, she led him out of his stall.

"All ready for our ride, Rosie?" Jess called out.

"Yes, Jess," Rosie answered, despondently. "Who's taking it out?" she asked.

"Sam," Jess answered.

"Great," Rosie muttered under her breath. "Just the person I was trying to get away from." She shrugged her shoulders. "Oh well."

"Do you need any help?" she called to Susannah, the little girl struggling with Horace.

"No, I think I can manage," Susannah answered. "I tacked him up myself," she added proudly as she led the pony to the mounting block and scrambled on. Rosie smiled absently.

"All ready?" Sam called impatiently as Hector pawed the ground.

Rosie followed on at the back as Sam led the ride out through the gate into the fields. Pepper sniffed the air excitedly.

"OK Susannah?" she called to the little girl ahead of her.

"Fine," Susannah answered, bumping along on Horace as they trotted through the fields.

"Let's start with a canter," said Sam, turning around to face the group. "All meet up by the corner of that field," he pointed.

Rosie looked uncertainly at Susannah. She had thought it was supposed to be a gentle, leisurely ride.

"How about a canter Susannah?" Rosie asked.

"Yes," she cried. "Great."

"Well follow on after the others then," Rosie said. "I'll go last."

Susannah circled Horace and nudged him on with her heels.

"You'll have to give him a little kick. Wake him up," Rosie shouted. Horace was liable to be a little sluggish if he wasn't pushed. Rosie had found that out the hard way. She'd learned to ride on him herself and many times she had found herself defending him until she had been forced to admit that maybe he was a little lazy.

Pepper was a much more responsive ride. He didn't even hesitate as Rosie asked him to canter. Rosie's eyes watered as the wind bit into her face. The horses ahead of her were a blur. Susannah looked as though she was sitting at an angle as they raced on.

Rosie gasped. Susannah *was* sitting at an angle – Horace's saddle was coming off! As Susannah slipped down his side, she clung onto his mane for dear life.

"Help, please help!" Susannah wailed pitifully.

Rosie didn't stop to think. All she knew was that they had to be stopped. Digging her heels into Pepper's side she pushed him forward, urging him on and on. The sweat rose on Pepper's neck as she pounded forward until they were neck and neck with the cantering horse. Leaning perilously out of the saddle, Rosie grabbed Horace's reins and they swerved to the right. It was too late. As Horace slowed to a trot, Susannah bounced to the ground in bumps. Rosie swung the pony around, drawing him to a halt as she made her way over to where Susannah was slowly scrambling to her feet. Unaware of the disturbance, Sam and the others had cantered on.

"Are you OK?" Rosie called.

"Yes Rosie," Susannah said weakly. "I'm all right really," she said bravely.

Rosie jumped off Pepper and walked over to the little girl. She was shaking from head to foot.

"You're not all right, are you?" Rosie said stroking her shoulder. "You're a little shaken, aren't you?"

"A little," Susannah trembled.

"Try stretching your limbs. Do you hurt anywhere?" Rosie asked.

"No, I don't think so."

Rosie breathed a sigh of relief. No broken bones this time.

"Did you tighten the girth up correctly?" she asked gently.

"Yes I did. I definitely did," Susannah protested. "I double checked it too. It was really tight. I don't know how it could have come undone."

"Don't worry," Rosie said, seeing Susannah's distress. She didn't want to press her. This was the kind of thing that could destroy someone's nerve and she was such a promising little rider.

"We'll go get the saddle and you can hop back on," Rosie said calmly. "We'll go back to the stables, but we ought to wait for the others to come back or they'll worry. There they are now."

In no time at all, Sam had thundered over to join the two of them.

"What on earth is going on?" he cried, seeing Rosie holding Horace's reins.

"The saddle came off, Sam," Rosie called.

"The saddle? You stupid girl," Sam shouted, turning to Susannah. "You must not have tightened the girth enough. I might have known you wouldn't be able to manage something like that on your own."

Rosie winced at his harsh words.

"I'm s-s-orry, Sam," Susannah whimpered. "I was so sure I had."

Rosie was furious. A reprimand was the last thing the little girl needed.

"Come on Susannah. I'll go back to the stables with you," she said, giving Sam a filthy look.

"Did you have to do that?" she said to Sam as Susannah turned away. "She took a heavy enough tumble as it was."

"I won't tolerate you talking to me like that, Rosie," Sam said in a harsh whisper. "She has to learn. Take her back to the stables and get her cleaned up. We don't want her mother seeing her like that. And I'll see *you* later." Without another word, he turned Hector in the direction they had just come from. "Come on everyone," he barked.

Jess looked embarrassed as she turned Minstrel to join the others. "Rosie, are you OK to go back with Susannah?" she asked her friend.

"I'll be fine," said Rosie. "You go on ahead. We'll manage. The ride's been spoiled for me anyway."

Jess smiled apologetically and turned to catch up with the others.

"Come on Susannah. Don't listen to that awful man," Rosie said, turning to the little girl. "When I had just started learning to ride, I put the saddle on the wrong way around, imagine that." It wasn't true, but at least it brought a smile to Susannah's face as they walked off in the direction of the saddle.

"There it is." Rosie pointed to where the saddle had landed. "Can you go and get it while I hold onto Horace and Pepper?"

"Sure." Susannah rushed over and picked it up as Rosie gazed into the distance. She could just see Minstrel's hindquarters as the last of the horses entered Larkfield Copse.

"Rosie, Rosie, quickly, come here."

Rosie's thoughts were disturbed by Susannah's pitiful cry.

"Look," Susannah cried, excitedly. "I knew it wasn't my fault. I knew I'd fastened it right. Look what I just found under the saddle flap."

Rosie looked at what Susannah was showing her and gasped. The girth had snapped in two.

"It must have been a rotten girth if it broke this

easily," Susannah was saying. "They're dangerous."

"You're right," said Rosie, edging over to where Susannah was standing. "Can I just take a look at that?"

"Of course," said Susannah.

"Well, we can't ride back now," said Rosie, looking at the girth. "If you can hold the saddle in place on Horace's back, I'll lead the horses back."

"OK Rosie." The little girl chattered away, seemingly having forgotten her fall.

"Now, do you think you could groom Horace when we get back?" Rosie asked as they walked along.

"Of course I can," Susannah grinned.

Rosie smiled at her enthusiasm and, as they reached the last field, she opened the gate to let them through.

"If you could lead these two back to their stalls, I'll take the saddle," Rosie said quickly.

"OK," said Susannah.

Rosie took the saddle and hurried into the tack room. Once alone, she closed the door and had a good look at the girth. It was just as she thought, although she hadn't wanted to admit it in front of Susannah. Girths didn't just snap in two. This one had been cut... and very deliberately cut. It must have been hanging by a thread when Susannah tacked up. But who could have done it? Rosie felt the hairs rising on the back of her neck. Her stomach was tying itself in knots.

Thoughts jostled around in her mind as she crossed the stables. She couldn't believe how many things had gone wrong in the couple of weeks that Nick and Sarah had been gone. She needed time to think. But time was the one thing she didn't have at the moment. There was something gnawing at her, right at the back of her mind. Something that held the key to it all. Something to do with the letter. But what was it?

And then it came to her, as clear as crystal. Rosie stopped in her tracks. Why hadn't any of them thought of it before? She could save Pepper yet. She smiled to herself. She had to speak to Beth.

"Hey, what are you doing back so early?" Alex called, appearing from Hector's box.

"Susannah took a tumble. Do you think you could look after her?" Rosie said, speeding off down the drive.

"Sure," said Alex. "But where are you going?"

"I'll tell you when I get back," Rosie said mysteriously. " Just tell Sam that I've gone home for lunch. Cover for me if you can."

"OK," Alex said and, before he could stop her, Rosie had done a quick about-face.

"Rosie." Alex's voice rang out hollowly.

But Rosie didn't reply. She didn't want to tell Alex what she was doing. She didn't want to tell him where she was going. This was something she wanted to do by herself... something she had to do alone.

9

A CHILLING DISCOVERY

Rosie's stomach rumbled as she jogged up the drive to Beth's house. It was the first time she had felt hungry in days. It must be a good sign.

Rosie gulped as she stood on the doorstep. It was vital that she explain everything correctly and she wasn't sure she knew where to begin.

"Double bookings, reduced earnings, Whisp's lameness, the missing saddle, the Tentenden entry form, the letter, the severed girth." Rosie said it all aloud, counting the points off on her fingers. It was all there. There was only one thing she couldn't explain – the reason why.

Beth would know what they should do, how to go about things. Rosie took a deep breath and reached out for the brass door knocker, rapping it hard against the old oak door. Clank!

Rosie waited patiently. For a moment, she was

worried there wouldn't be anyone at home, but then she heard the sound of feet padding along carpet. Rosie breathed a sigh of relief as Beth's mother answered the door.

"Hello, Mrs. Wilson. Is Beth here please?"

"Oh Rosie, it's you." Beth's mother smiled. "Beth was wondering when you'd come to see her."

"How is she?" Rosie asked quietly.

"Oh, much better. Another few weeks and she'll be back at Sandy Lane with you," said Mrs. Wilson, leading the way into the sitting room where Beth was sitting on the sofa.

"Rosie." Beth grinned warmly. "At last. I thought you'd forgotten me. Hang on a minute. I'll turn off the video."

Beth was right. It was the first time that any of them had visited her. Rosie felt embarrassed. She hadn't even come to ask Beth about her leg either.

"You look worried," said Beth. "Come and sit down and tell me your news. How are things at the stables? How are the new people fitting in?"

"That's sort of what I've come to talk to you about," Rosie said desperately. "It's not good. I need your help."

"Why, what is it?" Beth asked, concerned. "There isn't anything wrong is there?"

"I'm not sure." Rosie took a deep breath. "I think I'd better start at the beginning."

Beth propped herself up as Rosie started to go through everything that had happened, trying to explain it all as clearly as possible, until she came to the letter.

"And when I got to Sandy Lane this morning there

was a letter from Nick and Sarah asking Sam to sell Pepper," she said breathlessly.

"What?" Beth gasped. "Nick would never sell him, not Pepper."

"I know, and that's when I started thinking... I don't think the letter's from Nick at all," Rosie continued excitedly.

"Well, who's it from then?" Beth asked, bemused.

Rosie stopped to draw breath.

"Well, I think Sam might have sent it himself. You see, it's typewritten to begin with. Why would Nick have typed a letter to Sam? It doesn't make any sense." Rosie didn't wait for an answer before she went on.

"That got me thinking. The letter said that Pepper had to be sold to cover all of the extra costs at the stables... feed bills, vet bills, farrier bills – that sort of stuff. Fine. But one thing that was included as an added expense was Blackjack's saddle – the one I told you about."

"Yes," said Beth. "I bet it's going to be really expensive."

"It is," said Rosie. "But don't you see, Beth? Nick and Sarah couldn't have known about it. We only ordered it yesterday and a letter takes more than a day to arrive from Kentucky!"

Beth let out a low whistle.

"So even if Sam and Vanessa *had* phoned Nick about the saddle, a letter still couldn't have gotten here in that time. So the letter can't be genuine, can it?" she said, slowly rising to her feet. "I think I'd better come to the stables with you and find out what's going on." She reached for her crutches. "I'll see if Mom will drive us there. Where did Sam and Vanessa come from anyway? And whatever happened to Dick Bryant? What did Nick tell you about them?" Beth's questions tumbled out one after the other.

"I don't know," said Rosie. "We haven't spoken to Nick since he left. In fact, you're the only one who has."

"I haven't spoken to Nick," said Beth.

"Yes you have," said Rosie, "when you called and told him about your accident."

"But I didn't call him, *you guys* did," said Beth.

"We... we didn't phone." Rosie's cry was strangled in her throat and her face drained of all color as she grasped the enormity of what they were saying. The two girls looked at each other in shock. If none of them had phoned Nick and Sarah, then who had? Unless... unless Sam and Vanessa hadn't been sent by Nick and Sarah at all.

Rosie felt a shiver run down her spine.

* * * * * * * * * * * * * * * *

Beth and Rosie discussed how to work things out on the car ride to Sandy Lane and began to make a plan.

"I'd better arrive after you, Rosie. I've got to appear to be coming by on the off-chance – just to see how things are going," said Beth.

"OK. I'll go on ahead of you when we get there," said Rosie. "And we really must call Nick and Sarah tonight."

"But how can we get hold of them?" said Beth. "You said the number had gone."

"You must have a copy of it though, haven't you?" Rosie said pleadingly.

"Well, no... I don't, Rosie," Beth said sheepishly. "I never jotted it down from the bulletin board. I didn't think I'd need it."

"Oh Beth," Rosie wailed. "What are we going to do? We can't ask Sam and Vanessa for the number. Even if they do have it, they'll never give it to us. Should we go to the police?"

"No, we've got to find out what they're up to for ourselves first," said Beth. "Who's going to believe us when we don't even know that?"

"You're right," said Rosie.

Mrs. Wilson dropped the girls off at the bottom of Sandy Lane and Rosie set off up the drive. A few minutes later, Beth hobbled into the yard, where she was immediately surrounded by excited faces and greeted with question after question.

"Beth, how's your leg?"

"Have you missed us?"

"Are you back for good?"

Beth smiled wearily. "Not exactly," she said. "I'd be pretty useless with this thing, wouldn't I?" she said, pointing to the white plaster cast on her leg. "I've just come to see how you're doing."

"Not that great," said Kate, gloomily. "The earnings have been down all this week."

"Where are Sam and Vanessa?" Rosie interrupted.

"Away again," Tom said gloomily. "There was a telephone call. They had to rush off... said they'd be back in an hour."

"I wonder where they've gone," Rosie said.

"Does it matter?" asked Jess.

"It might," Rosie said mysteriously.

"Rosie and I have got something to tell you about our friends Sam and Vanessa," Beth explained.

"Something important?" Tom asked.

"Well." Rosie took a deep breath. "I think we'd better go somewhere more private. Just in case they come back."

"Don't keep us in suspense," said Tom. "Tell us."

Quickly, they all hurried to the tack room.

"I don't know where to begin," Rosie said, looking at the faces turned toward her.

"Start at the beginning... like you did with me," Beth said encouragingly.

"OK," said Rosie.

And she took a deep breath and began the story at the very beginning... starting with her misgivings about Sam and Vanessa, glossing over the incidents they all knew about already, right through to the letter.

There was a great deal of commotion as her story unfolded.

"Go on Rosie," said Beth. "Tell them about the significance of the phone call, or rather the non-phone call."

Amid gasps of horror, Rosie told them how Beth hadn't phoned Nick and Sarah.

"But neither did we," Tom gasped.

"Then where have Sam and Vanessa come from?" Kate burst out.

"That's what we've got to find out," Beth said in a calm voice.

"I think we should phone Nick and Sarah," Tom said sensibly.

Rosie and Beth exchanged nervous glances.

"We can't, Tom," said Rosie.

"Of course we can, Rosie. I know we decided not to bother them before, but this is an emergency. They'd want to know."

"You don't understand, Tom," said Rosie. "There's something I haven't told you... last night, after you left, I was going to phone them. Do you remember?"

"Of course I do," said Tom.

"Well, I couldn't," Rosie said gloomily. "When I got to the tack room, the number had gone and Beth hasn't got a copy of it."

"Oh no," said Tom, holding his head in his hands. "What can we do? Who can we tell?"

"We should go to the police," said Kate.

"And say what?" said Rosie. The others all looked worried.

"Look everyone," said Beth. "Rosie and I have thought all this through. If you'd just give us a chance to explain, we'll tell you our plan."

The others all nodded in agreement.

"Well," said Beth. "We don't have any answers at the moment, so we have to tread very carefully to get them. We don't want Sam and Vanessa getting wind that something's up and we can't go around accusing them of anything until we know what's going on."

"But we're back at school Monday," Tom said. "Who'll look after the stables? Nick and Sarah aren't back until Saturday. Who knows what could happen in a week!"

"I don't propose that we sit tight for long," said

Beth. "Just until we can find out what they're up to. And if you introduce me to them, I'll offer to help out while you're all at school. I know I won't be much good around the grounds, but they'll need someone to take bookings. I can keep an eye on things then."

"But what if they don't agree to it?" said Jess.

Beth laughed grimly. "By the sound of it, I don't think they're going to turn down the offer of free help, do you?"

"You're right," said Tom.

"OK. So that's decided. Are we all agreed?" Beth asked, turning to the group.

"Yes," everyone answered.

"But what about Pepper?" Rosie asked. "He's supposed to be sold on Friday. If we don't put a stop to Sam and Vanessa soon, he'll be gone before we know it."

"We'll just have to take him ourselves and hide him somewhere," said Beth.

"Where?" asked Rosie.

"There's Mr. Green's pig farm?" Tom suggested. "It's near enough to the stables, but no one would think to look in one of those crumbly, old outbuildings at the back."

"Good idea," Kate and Alex said in unison.

"But what if Sam and Vanessa call the police?" said Tom. "What if they report Pepper as stolen?"

"I don't think they'll do that Tom, do you?" said Beth. "I think they'll want to avoid the police at all costs. But it's a gamble we'll have to take. Now, isn't that a car? We'd better break this up. And remember everyone, try to behave as normally as possible." Slowly, everyone filed out of the tack room.

"Hi Sam, hi Vanessa," Tom called, trying to act cheerfully. "We've got a visitor."

Sam stepped out of the car to face him, looking puzzled.

"Meet Beth, our stable girl," Tom said, as Beth stepped out of the tack room. Rosie watched Sam's face for a reaction. He must be a better actor than she thought for, although he looked surprised, he was quick to collect his composure and stretched out his hand.

"Hi Beth," he said, stepping out of the car. "Pleased to meet you. Heard all about your terrible accident. How's the leg then?" he asked.

"Oh fine. N-n-not bad," she stuttered.

Rosie watched the color drain from Beth's face. If she wasn't careful she'd be the one to give the game away. They were all supposed to act as though nothing was wrong and Beth was being all jumpy.

As if able to read Rosie's thoughts, Beth managed to regain her composure in time to make her offer of organizing the bookings.

"That's very kind of you," said Sam. "We could do with some help around here too. We'll be rushed off our feet with our regulars back at school." He grinned.

"Well, I am getting a little bored at home too," Beth smiled weakly. "I can't stand being away from the stables."

"That's settled then," said Sam. "Now, what do we have scheduled this afternoon?" he asked.

"You're giving a lesson at three, Sam," Tom answered. "I'll make a start on getting the horses tacked up."

"Fine. Well, I'll get a cup of coffee at the house and then I'll join you."

"And I'll help you with Pepper, Rosie," said Beth, forcing a frozen smile in Sam's direction.

"You don't have to," Rosie said surprised. "Why don't you sit down and rest your leg? You look tired."

"No, I'd like to," Beth said forcefully, following her over to his stall.

Rosie drew back the bolt and let them inside. Beth closed the door behind her and let out a huge sigh. Leaning against the wall, she looked as though she'd had the wind knocked out of her.

"What's up? What is it Beth? You look like you've seen a ghost," Rosie said. "You're really pale. You almost gave us away out there. Are you sure you're going to be all right here on your own next week?"

"Yes, I'll be fine. It's not that, Rosie. I've just had a shock, that's all. You see, I recognize Sam."

Rosie frowned. "Where from?" she asked.

Beth took a deep breath. "If I'm not mistaken, Sam was the driver of that car... the one that almost ran me down."

"What!" Rosie gasped. "The red sports car? Are you sure?"

"I'm sure," said Beth. "There's no doubt about it. Sam was definitely driving. Rosie, he could have killed me!"

10

MIDNIGHT RIDE

Rosie stared at Beth in horror. If Sam had no qualms about running someone down, then just what would he stop at? Rosie shuddered. Things were slowly starting to fall into place – Sam and Vanessa knowing so much about the accident; the way they had arrived so promptly; all of the disasters that had struck. The pieces of the jigsaw were beginning to come together. And Rosie wasn't too sure she liked the picture.

"All right in there girls?" Rosie jumped as Sam's face loomed over the stall door.

"Yes, fine," she said returning his clear, calculated gaze.

Beth couldn't bring herself to look at him.

"Beth, we've got to get Pepper out of here right away," Rosie whispered urgently once Sam had walked away.

"We'll have to be careful, Rosie," Beth breathed.

"We can't take him too soon or we won't find out what they're up to and we won't stand a chance with the police. Who's going to believe us? It all sounds so ridiculous."

"But can't you tell them that Sam was driving that car?" Rosie said desperately.

"But I said in my statement that I couldn't remember what the man looked like. And it was true. It was only seeing him today that jogged my memory. It's going to look very strange if I suddenly come up with the perfect picture."

"It certainly doesn't look that good," Rosie said thoughtfully. "But we can't hang on for much longer."

"No," said Beth. "But we have to try to get some evidence... see if Sam and Vanessa let anything slip. After all, at the moment, we don't even know what they're up to. It's probably best if you take Pepper on Thursday evening."

Rosie gulped. "Isn't that cutting it a little close? Someone's coming to pick him up on Friday."

"No," said Beth firmly, "not if I keep an eye on things here. And I'll phone you if there's any news."

"OK," said Rosie hesitantly. "Thursday it is, then."

* * * * * * * * * * * * * * * * *

Beth was as good as her word and kept everyone informed about the goings-on at the stables, but there wasn't a great deal to report and the next few days passed slowly for Rosie. Concentrating on schoolwork was near impossible. She couldn't help but worry that something terrible was happening in her absence. She was sure that Sam and Vanessa must be planning some grand finale before Nick and Sarah returned.

When Beth phoned on Thursday evening, Rosie was shaking so much she could hardly hold the receiver.

"All set Rosie?" Beth whispered. "I can't talk very loudly. My mother's lurking in the background. Do you have it all mapped out for tonight?"

"Yes," Rosie answered. "Yes, I've set my alarm for eleven thirty."

"And you know exactly where you're taking Pepper?"

"Yes, the old shed to the right of the huge barn. It's all figured out," said Rosie.

"Well, good luck then."

Rosie put down the phone and looked at her watch. Nine o'clock. Eleven thirty seemed like an eternity.

"Are you all right, Rosie?" her mother asked. "You look a little pale. You're not about to come down with something are you?"

"No Mom," Rosie said. "But I think I'll go off to bed and get a good night's sleep."

"OK." Rosie's mother smiled. "Good night then."

Rosie padded up the stairs and closed the door behind her. Quickly, she double-checked she had everything: flashlight, pony treats, riding hat. Yes, that was everything.

Pacing up and down the room, she set her alarm clock and pulled out her britches from the closet. Climbing into bed, Rosie turned on the bedside lamp and picked up her latest pony book. But five pages later, she realized she hadn't taken in any of the story. It was no good. Turning out the lamp, she snuggled under her comforter.

Drifting in and out of sleep, she woke up to see the luminous hands on her alarm clock at eleven twenty. Swiftly, she turned it off before it could make a noise. Creeping out of bed, she threw off her pajamas and pulled a sweater on over her head as she gathered up her things. Stopping for a moment to plump up her pillows and put them under her comforter, she tiptoed out onto the landing. Her heart was racing and her legs felt like jelly. Easing her way down to the hallway, careful to avoid the creaky stair, she drew back the bolt on the front door and stepped outside.

The cold was the first thing that hit her as she hurried over to her bike. It was a clear night and there wasn't anyone in sight. Nimbly, she rode out of the driveway, and down the dimly-lit roads. As she headed into the dead of the night, the trees cast their shadowy silhouettes on the ground. Rosie reached Sandy Lane in no time at all.

Jumping to the ground, she wheeled her bike off the drive and hid it in the hedgerow. Taking a quick glance up the drive, she was surprised to see the house all lit up. A hazy yellow glow surrounded it. She knew she should go straight to Pepper's stall, but she found herself inextricably drawn toward the light in the house. She couldn't stop herself. What would Sam and Vanessa do if they caught her? Rosie shuddered at the thought.

Ducking down, she stole up on the house, like a lion stalking its prey, and peered into the living room. Inside, Sam sat twirling a silver cigarette lighter in his fingers. The smoke from his cigarette spiraled out of the open window. Rosie strained her ears to hear what they were saying.

"I should never have listened to this crazy scheme. You're taking things too far, Ralph." It was Vanessa's voice.

What were they talking about? Rosie froze to the spot. She took a long look through the window. She could only see Sam and Vanessa inside, so where was Ralph? Unless...

Rosie strained her ears to listen to the continuing conversation. The words that followed sent shivers down her spine. Her heart began to palpitate.

"...I haven't gone far enough, that's the problem," Sam was saying. "I told you we wouldn't be able to ruin Sandy Lane's reputation with double bookings and canceled rides. Nick Brooks – damn him – he's back on Saturday and time's running out. I've got to do something serious... something to destroy Sandy Lane, once and for all."

Rosie staggered back, stumbling into the bush behind her.

"Who's that, who's there?" Sam called, opening the door to the house.

Rosie felt the hairs rising on the back of her neck. Could he see her? He seemed to be looking straight through her. Her pulse was racing. She couldn't breathe. She felt herself burning up.

"There's no one there. You're imagining things," Vanessa's voice whined. "Come on back inside. We ought to get some sleep. We've got a lot to do over the next couple of days. Pepper's being picked up tomorrow, isn't he? What have you done about payment?"

"Cash on delivery, that was the deal," said Sam, walking into the kitchen and out of earshot.

Rosie was frozen to the spot. Scrunching herself up into a ball, she sat tight. What did it all mean? What terrible thing did they have planned for Sandy Lane?

She looked at her watch. Half past twelve. How long would she have to wait until the coast was clear to get Pepper? Gingerly, she stood up and looked through the window. Sam was sitting up poring over some papers. Would he never go to bed? She was starting to feel the cold now and the night air was numbing her fingers. She settled herself down again.

It was a good ten minutes before she saw one of the lights flicker off. Her heart leapt and slowly she raised herself to her feet. Vanessa was wandering around the room, switching the lamps off as she went. They must be going to bed. Rosie breathed a sigh of relief. She had made it undetected. She waited a few more minutes to give them time to get up the stairs and into bed, then stealthily she crept into the yard.

Pepper looked wide-eyed as Rosie drew back the bolt and stepped inside his stall.

"Ssh, ssh my boy. We've got to get you away from here quickly," she said, holding out the handful of pony treats she had brought with her.

Pepper munched contentedly as Rosie shone her light around the stall. Beth had been as good as her word and left the tack out for her. Deftly, Rosie put the bridle on over Pepper's head.

"Easy now," she whispered as she grabbed a haynet and slung it over her shoulder. There wasn't time for a saddle. She'd have to ride bareback.

Leading Pepper out of his stall, she turned him to the gate behind the stables. She was going to have to ride him to Mr. Green's pig farm across the fields, to avoid passing the house. With a quick backward glance, Rosie vaulted onto the little pony's back. She half-expected to hear an angry yell as she nudged Pepper forward into a trot. But all was quiet.

The farther Rosie rode from Sandy Lane, the more confident she felt. Cantering through the fields, they crossed the old coastal track and headed into Bucknell Woods.

It was dark, but Rosie could vaguely see her way by the light of the moon. The sound of a hooting owl stopped Pepper in his tracks, but Rosie was quick to nudge him on. The smell of pine clung to the air as they picked their way through the trees.

"We're nearly there, Pepper," she said, more to reassure herself than anything else.

All was quiet as they walked out of the woods and crossed the road. This was the part where they had to be careful. If Sam had heard them leave Sandy Lane, he would be bound to come searching by car. But Rosie could hear neither the sound of a car engine nor see the flash of headlights. She started to relax as they trotted across the pavement.

Taking the back route into Mr. Green's pig farm, she headed straight for the shed.

"No one will think to look for you here, Pepper," she whispered, jumping to the ground. "I know it's not what you're used to, but you'll be safe," she went on, as she took off his bridle and shut the little pony in. "I'm going to have to leave you now – before anyone notices that I'm missing. You'll be all right, really you will." She scattered the last of the pony treats on the floor and attached the haynet to a ring. "And Jess is going to come and see you tomorrow morning before school, with your breakfast." She patted his speckled shoulder fondly.

Pepper snickered softly as Rosie filled the trough with water. She wished she could stay all night to keep guard over him. But there were other things she had to do. She must be up early to call everyone and tell them her awful discovery. They needed to make plans. With a heavy heart, Rosie headed for home.

11

PLANS

"Sam's furious. He's been running around cursing, accusing everyone imaginable of taking Pepper." Beth laughed on the phone to Rosie. "You should have seen his face. He looked absolutely livid. You're top on his list of suspects by the way."

"Beth," Rosie said quietly.

"And I double-bluffed him too," Beth continued, not stopping to listen. "Asked him why he didn't call the police. But it's just as we thought. He didn't want to."

"*Beth*," Rosie pleaded urgently. "Would you just stop and listen. You're not going to believe it. I overheard Sam and Vanessa talking at the house last night... the double bookings, the canceled rides... they planned it all. It was all done on purpose, to ruin Sandy Lane's reputation," she said breathlessly.

There was no answer from the other end as Beth

listened to what Rosie was saying.

"Beth... can you hear me? Are you still there?"

"Yes, yes," Beth said. "I'm still here. But why? Why would they want to ruin Sandy Lane's reputation? It doesn't make any sense."

"I don't know why, Beth," Rosie said. "But from the way they were talking they're certainly not friends of Nick and Sarah's." Rosie took a deep breath. "It gets worse. They know that Nick and Sarah are back on Saturday, and they're planning to do something else... something more serious. Sam talked about destroying Sandy Lane once and for all. What can he mean?"

"I don't know," Beth said hesitantly. "I'm scared to think. Rosie, are you sure you heard things right?"

"Very sure," said Rosie. "We've got to go to the police, Beth. Now... this is getting out of control."

"But what do we tell them, Rosie? What do we say? That you overheard a conversation at the house in the middle of the night? They'll never believe us. We need proof of exactly what Sam and Vanessa are up to. Look, Nick and Sarah are due back tomorrow aren't they?

"Yes," Rosie said slowly.

"Then we'll just have to sit tight and keep watch. Whatever Sam and Vanessa have planned, they've got to do it soon. And we must be there to stop them. If we can get firm evidence, then we can go to the police. Listen, you go to school and I'll think of a plan. Do you think you can get everyone to meet me at eight this evening at the bottom of the driveway?" Beth said quickly. "We can't leave Sandy Lane unguarded for a moment.

"Yes," said Rosie. "I'm sure I can pass the word on

to everyone at school."

"Good," Beth said.

"But Beth," Rosie said uncertainly. "What if we can't stop them?"

There was no answer, as Beth stopped to think.

"We will, Rosie," she answered grimly. "We just have to."

* * * * * * * * * * * * * * * * *

It was dusk when everyone met up at the bottom of the drive and the twilight cast an eerie haze around the group of figures. Alex and Kate stood huddled up inside their jackets as Charlie shuffled his feet. Tom held a flashlight, lighting up Jess's pinched features. They had been horrified when Rosie had told them what she had overheard.

"Is everyone here?" Beth asked, looking around her. They all nodded.

"OK," she went on. "We've got to decide on a plan of action. We don't know exactly what Sam and Vanessa are going to do, but whatever it is, we've got to catch them red-handed. We'll have to keep an eye on them every minute of the day until Nick and Sarah get back... that means we can't leave Sandy Lane unguarded at any time, starting with tonight."

"But what do we tell our parents?" Rosie said, worried.

Beth bit her lip nervously. "I don't think we should

tell our parents anything – not yet."

Rosie looked anxious. "OK then," she said slowly.

"I think we should make the tack room, the barn, the house, the outdoor arena and the three rows of stalls all look-out points," said Beth. "Is everyone happy with that?"

"Yes," they all answered.

"Well, there are seven of us," Beth went on. "At the first sign of trouble, we have to hold them and call the police. Is everyone agreed?"

Everyone nodded in acceptance.

"Now," said Beth. "Remember, no one is to raise the alarm until they are absolutely certain Sam and Vanessa are up to something. They should have finished the evening feeding by now. My guess is that they'll be in the house packing up their stuff, so make sure you get to your positions without being seen."

Beth was right. As Rosie crept behind the stables, she could see the silhouetted figures of Sam and Vanessa moving around inside the house. Their Suburban was parked close to the house, its back wide open as they stacked their stuff in for their getaway. Rosie was furious to see Nick's silver racing trophies piled up with all the other things in the back, but something told her that this wasn't the worst they could expect. She couldn't resist pausing by the house to listen to Sam and Vanessa's conversation as she made her way to the barn. They were arguing. Rosie felt pleased when she realized that her handiwork was the cause of their distress.

"We can't wait any longer for Pepper to show up," Sam was saying. "It's a nuisance. We desperately needed that money. I'm sure those horrible children must have taken him. If only I could think where." He scratched his head.

"We can't worry about that now," said Vanessa. "It's more important that we clear out of here quickly. Things are starting to get a little uncomfortable for my liking."

As much as she would have liked to have stayed and listened, Rosie dragged herself along to the big barn. As she crept along the path, she heard Feather let out a loud whinny, but apart from that, all was quiet.

Climbing on top of the hay bales, she settled herself down. She knew she was in for a long wait and she was tired. She hadn't gotten to bed until two in the morning and she'd been up at seven for school. She had to stay awake. Desperately, she tried to keep her eyes open, but her head kept rolling back. What had Beth said? No one was to raise the alarm until they were certain... absolutely certain. Rosie yawned. The light wasn't good in the stables at the moment. She was losing her concentration.

Rosie looked at her watch. Eight thirty. She shifted her body as she cast her mind back to all that had happened. There was something bothering her. If only she could think straight...

Rosie leaned back, the words from last night ringing in her ears. Ralph... Ralph... Ralph.

She must have dozed off because, when she awoke, there was a loud commotion going on in the yard. A strong acrid smell permeated the air. She drew her breath in sharply. What was it ? It smelled like a garage... It was gasoline, that's what it was! Peering over the top of the hay bales, she saw Sam and Vanessa carrying large cans across the yard. Rosie started to panic as she scrambled out of the hay. Fire! They had meant exactly what they had said. They did mean to destroy Sandy Lane once and for all – Sam and Vanessa planned to burn the stables to the ground. Rosie's heart sank. Had she and her friends arrived too late?

Rosie felt sickened. What did Sam and Vanessa think would happen to all of the horses? Did they plan to let them go up in smoke? Rosie went hot and cold at the thought. She was rooted to the spot. Her feet felt like leaden weights.

"What can I do?" she croaked.

But before she had time to do anything at all, she saw Tom step out from the shadows and shout across the yard.

"Just stop right there." His voice echoed around the stables.

* * * * * * * * * * * * * * * * *

Sam seemed startled for a moment and then he saw who it was and started to laugh.

"So you think you're going to stop me do you, Tom?" he jeered.

Rosie grimaced as beams of light bounced off the silver object in Sam's hand. It was the cigarette lighter she had seen him playing with before. One flick of the wrist was all that was needed to destroy Sandy Lane. With all the gas Sam and Vanessa had used to lace the stables, Sandy Lane wouldn't stand a chance.

Sam smiled sneeringly, flicking the lid of the lighter up and down while he waited for Tom's next move.

Rosie held her breath. If Tom didn't act quickly, Sandy Lane would go up in smoke. She had to do something herself.

"Yes, we can put a stop to you," Rosie called from her hiding place. "We know what your game is. Deliberate sabotage... isn't that what it's called? I think the police will be very interested in what we have to say."

Sam laughed a low, menacing laugh.

"So you think the police will believe you kids, do you? By the time they've heard your version of events, Sandy Lane will be history and we'll be out of here without a trace."

"You may be out of here, but we'll know where to find you, Ralph... Ralph Winterson," Rosie said bravely.

Sam looked startled.

"Isn't that your real name, Sam?" Rosie went on, stronger now. "You're nothing but an imposter – Ralph Winterson of the Clarendon Equestrian Center, although you never do any work there either. You've been cited for cruelty to horses too, haven't you?"

Tom let out a loud gasp. For a moment there was silence. And then the stillness was broken by a loud clapping sound.

"Very good, my dear."

Sneeringly, Sam clapped his hands together in mock applause.

"You've certainly done your homework. But you can't prove a word of it. Can you?" he challenged.

"Can't I?" Rosie said calmly. "But I can. You see, I

have evidence to prove it – a taped conversation between you and Vanessa about twelve thirty last night, talking about the double bookings and canceled rides. Does it ring any bells?" she demanded. "I think the police will believe us then."

"You're bluffing," said Sam. But from the look on his face, Rosie knew that he wasn't sure.

"OK," he said, changing his tactics. "What do you want? Money?"

Rosie looked at him disgusted.

"The only thing we want is to get you away from here before Nick and Sarah come back. Did you really think you could ruin Sandy Lane's reputation so easily? Did you really think everyone would flock to your lousy stables?"

"Well, if we do as you say, what will you do with the tape?" Sam's voice reverberated around the yard.

"Nothing," said Rosie calmly, "on one condition..."

The others all looked at her in amazement.

Tom seemed about to say something, but Rosie held up her hand to silence him and swallowed hard.

"We won't do anything, so long as you agree to close down the Clarendon Equestrian Center without any fuss. Pack your bags and disappear out of this neighborhood for good."

Sam opened his mouth to speak and closed it again. Realizing he was beaten, he shut up his lighter with a final snap and turned to go.

"And one more thing," Rosie called sharply. "You can put Nick's racing trophies back in the house where you found them."

Sam shot her an angry glance and turned to Vanessa.

"Come on," he growled. "We're out of here. We've

got better things to do."

Everything had happened so quickly. One minute, Sam held the future of Sandy Lane in his hand, the next, he and Vanessa had shut up the back of their Suburban and were speeding out of the yard.

"I hope that's the last we'll see of them," said Rosie.

No one knew what to say and for a moment there was an uncomfortable silence until Jess burst out.

"Rosie, you were awesome," she said. "I can't believe you figured all that out for yourself."

"It wasn't that hard," Rosie said blushing graciously. "Just a little detective work."

"But to get it all on tape," Tom said admiringly.

"Well actually, I didn't." Rosie reddened and laughed. "I couldn't possibly have gotten anything clearly on tape from that distance. That was just a bluff."

12

ALL IS WELL

"So when Sam, or should I say Ralph, realized that he couldn't destroy Sandy Lane's reputation so easily, he turned to more drastic measures."

It was Saturday at Sandy Lane and the regulars had spent the morning hard at work, getting rid of all the gasoline-soaked straw. Susannah was listening to Rosie's story.

"So, that explains the *'For Sale'* board outside the Clarendon Equestrian Center," said Susannah. "Everyone's been talking about it."

Rosie smiled thoughtfully.

"But there's one thing I don't understand," Susannah went on. "Why didn't you go right to the police when you found out what they were up to?"

"Well," Rosie hesitated. "First, we didn't really know what they were up to until the very last minute, and secondly, I didn't have any evidence anyway. It

111

would have been my word against theirs."

"You're right," said Susannah.

"And what's more," Rosie said proudly, "I've just had some amazing news."

Rosie bent down and whispered something in the little girl's ear.

"Wow," said Susannah. "Tentenden! Wait till the others hear."

"What are you two whispering about?" asked Jess, coming up behind them. "Did I hear the word Tentenden mentioned?"

"You certainly did," said Rosie. "Guess what?" she said proudly, as everyone gathered around. "I can't keep it a secret any longer. We'll be riding in the Tentenden Team Chase next weekend after all. I phoned them this morning, just in time it appears." She grinned mischievously. "It seems one of the teams have dropped out, the Clarendon Equestrian Center, no less." Her eyes sparkled. "And we can take their place."

"What?" shrieked Tom.

"But that's fantastic, Rosie," Jess whooped, throwing her riding hat in the air.

Rosie beamed as she looked around at the delighted faces of her friends. In her dreams, the Tentenden trophy had long been theirs. She could almost see it now, the silver cup shimmering in the tack room.

But at that moment, everyone's excited chatter was silenced as a car rounded the corner and pulled up in the yard. Then there were voices. Voices they all recognized. Nick and Sarah had returned from Kentucky! Ebony went wild and hurled himself upon them as they stepped out of the taxi and everyone gathered around.

"Whoa boy, now calm down," Nick laughed. "Hi everyone," he said looking around him at the welcoming faces. "Whew. It's good to be home," he grinned. "I don't suppose much has happened here while we've been away, but have we got some stories for you."

Rosie looked at the others and smiled.

A Horse for the Summer by Michelle Bates

The first title in the Sandy Lane Stables series

There was a frantic whinny and the sound of drumming hooves reverberated around the stables as Chancey pranced down the ramp. He was certainly on his toes, but he didn't look like the sleek, well turned-out horse that Tom remembered seeing last season. He was still unclipped and his mangy winter coat was flecked with foam as feverishly he pawed the ground. No one knew what to say...

When Tom is loaned a prize-winning show jumper for the summer, things don't turn out quite as he hoped. Chancey is wild and unpredictable and Tom is forced to start training him in secret. But the days of summer are numbered and Chancey isn't Tom's to keep forever. At some point, he will have to give him back...

The Runaway Pony by Susannah Leigh

The second title in the Sandy Lane Stables series

Angry shouting and the crunch of hooves on gravel made Jess spin around sharply. Careening towards her, wild-eyed with fear and long tail flying behind, was a palomino pony. It was completely out of control. Jess's heart began to pound and her breath came in sharp gasps, but almost without thinking she held out her arms...

When the bridleless and riderless palomino pony clatters into the stables, no one is more surprised than Jess. Hot on the pony's hooves comes a man waving a halter. Jess helps him catch the pony and sends them on their way. Little is she to know what far-reaching consequences her simple actions will have...

The Midnight Horse by Michelle Bates

The fourth title in the Sandy Lane Stables series

The horse cantered gracefully around the paddock in long easy strides, his tail held high, the crest of his neck arched. His jet-black coat contrasted sharply with the white frost, his hooves hardly touching the ground as he danced forward.

Riding at the Hawthorn Horse Trials is all that Kate has dreamed of and this year she has a real chance of winning. As she works hard to prepare for the day, it seems nothing will distract her from her goal. But then the mysterious midnight horse rides into Kate's life, and suddenly everything changes...